HAUNTED LANDSCAPES

Also by Donald R. Rawe

Fiction

LOOKING FOR LOVE IN A GREAT CITY (novel)

THE MERMAID OF PADSTOW (stories and poems)

Occult

CORNISH HAUNTINGS AND HAPPENINGS

History and Topography

A PROSPECT OF CORNWALL

CORNISH VILLAGES

PADSTOW AND DISTRICT (with Jack Ingrey)

Folklore

TRADITIONAL CORNISH STORIES AND RHYMES

PADSTOW'S OBBY OSS AND MAYDAY FESTIVITIES

Plays

IN THE ROAR OF THE SEA (adapted from the novel by
    S. Baring Gould)

PETROC OF CORNWALL

THE TRIALS OF ST PIRAN

GERAINT, LAST OF THE ARTHURIANS

THE CREATION OF THE WORLD (translated from the
Cornish)

HAWKER OF MORWENSTOW

MURDER AT BOHELLAND

THE LAST VOYAGE OF ALFRED WALLIS

HAUNTED LANDSCAPES

Cornish and West Country Tales of the Supernatural

DONALD R. RAWE

Lodenek Press

ISBN 0946 143 22 6

Published by Lodenek Press, Portloe, Truro, Cornwall
(Tel) 0872 501736

Typeset by the Wordfactory, Rear Hawkins House, Barracks Ope, High Street, Falmouth, Cornwall (0326 313211)

Printed by St George Printing Works Ltd., Wilson Way, Pool, Redruth, Cornwall (0209 2170133)

ACKNOWLEDGEMENTS

Of the stories in this volume, two have been published previously: Night on Roughtor, in *Haunted Cornwall*, and In Killigarrek Wood, in *Cornish Ghost Stories*. Both these collections were edited by Denys Val Baker, who provided an outlet and encouragement to so many aspiring writers in Cornwall especially in his two series of the *Cornish Review*, and to whose memory this book is affectionately dedicated.

I am indebted to Mr. Jack Ingrey for the account of the psychic phenomena recorded at Harlyn House, near Padstow, in 1964, on which The Roskilly House Affair is based. I have used entirely fictional characters in this story; no living person is intentionally portrayed in it.

The basic story lines of The Heretic, The Homecoming and The Search for Perfection were provided by Mr. Len Sampson, to whom grateful acknowledgement is made.

A Skeleton in the Cupboard was first written as a one-act drama, and performed by the Kernow Players of Padstow in the Cornwall Area Drama Festival. It was awarded the prize for the best original script of its year by the British Theatre Association. The playscript is obtainable in *A Cornish Quintette* (Five One Act Plays from the Cornwall Drama Festivals), also published by Lodenek Press.

A Revenant is loosely based on the character and situation of Mrs Annie Simpson, a notable eccentric of Padstow, who for many years lived at Abbey House on the quayside there. It also makes use of a remarkable episode which most Padstow residents will remember: the proposal to open an amusement arcade, next to that charming listed building which is so valuable a feature of the port. Fortunately North Cornwall District Council refused planning permission, and an appeal was dismissed by the Department of the Environment's Inspector, who was clearly impressed by the whole town's massive and vociferous opposition to the proposal.

Finally, I must thank my wife for invaluable help in proof-correcting and editing this book.

D.R.R.
March 1994

In Memoriam

DENYS VAL BAKER

Author and Editor

1917-1984

Contents

THE ROSKILLY HOUSE AFFAIR

Roskilly House broods behind the oaks and beeches flanking its drive, which turns off a narrow lane near Gwyndreath Bay in North Cornwall. The house is a mixture of architectural styles, revealing the various purposes it served down the centuries: medieval monastic house, Tudor manor, Jacobean farmhouse, and, from Georgian times, a gentleman's residence. At the end of the last century a huge lantern light was built into the apex of its roof. Perhaps it is the screen of dark trees about it, including Cornish elms and Corsican pines to its rear, which gives the place its forbidding, secretive appearance; or perhaps it is the result of what it has witnessed over the years. As one approaches it from the lane, the rooks nesting in the tall boughs above look down and pass weird cabalistic warnings to each other. Before the house is the decaying stump of an immense cedar of Lebanon which once dominated the lawn.

The house was unoccupied for some ten years during the 1939-45 war, and was then bought for quite a modest sum by Professor Henry Hawken, who wanted a quiet retreat during college vacations: a place in the country where, in the best traditions of civilised and artistic people, he could study, write, and have down friends for long weekends and house parties.

Henry Hawken was a sound if hardly brilliant Cambridge don, who had built up a considerable reputation as an authority on the fine arts. His books *Aestheticism in Our Time, Nineteenth Century British Ceramics, The Architecture of the Restoration*, and many others, had sold for twenty years (mainly to libraries), and massively bored the public who thought they ought to read them. At the time of acquiring Roskilly, Henry was Professor of Fine Art, and had reached the age at which normally a man thinks of retiring. But being restless, curious, and insufferably self-important in all his dealings, he could not bring himself to believe that he had nothing more to say to the world.

Away from the university he sought, and found, various means of impressing audiences, somewhat less learned though they were than those he was used to addressing. Local Women's Institutes, Old Cornwall Societies, Arts clubs, and the august Royal Institution of Cornwall alike, heard the Professor hold forth on his favourite hobby-horse: how to tell what he considered good art from bad, what is wrong in modern art, and also, what is right – his own canons of aestheticism being rigidly defined. And once started, the Professor was difficult to stop. He was seldom invited twice to the same society or gathering.

It was Henry Hawken's wife Emma, who wrote poetry and books for children, who first heard, or felt, the presences at Roskilly. Listening to her account of them, the Professor smiled indulgently, indicating with a slight wrinkle of his eyebrows that they were figments of her fey imagination. Emma was quite used to having her notions dismissed more or less out of hand by Henry, though she never gave them up on that account. In time, her attitude seemed to imply, perhaps he would find out the truth. As, indeed, he did.

Christmas is a time of pause and quietude in Cornwall, and in the 1950s there was little entertainment to be had in that district beyond carol services with local hand-bell ringers, and sing-songs in the nearest pub, The Cornish Arms at St. Meva. Cinemas catered entirely for children, pantomimes similarly dominated the live theatres within reach; television (black and white) on BBC offered a profusion of panel games, football and variety acts. Therefore the Professor and Emma had invited a few friends down to stay over Christmas and New Year, to relieve the boredom and provide intelligent conversation. And in between tramping the footpaths along the cliffs, playing records of string quartets and Mozart symphonies, and a round or two of golf on the local links, the conversation was the chief delight of the company. There was also choice wine and very tolerable food cooked by the Professor's house-keeper, supervised by Emma, who produced her own Christmas pudding and some delicious sweets.

Ortford Entwistle, a middle-aged poet from the North of whom Henry Hawken approved (they had been under-graduates together at Trinity), was regarded as an entertaining and cynical personality, though somewhat too fond of drink and apt to become truculent in argument around midnight. Dr. Julius Natwich, an authority on industrial archaeology, was Director of a museum of steam engines, water-wheels and mining gear set up at Camborne; young, dark and unmarried, he was looked upon with great favour by the ladies of the company. H.J. Berkshaw, a Lancashire man who lived at St. Ives, was well-known for his series of popular historical novels set in nineteenth-century Cornwall, one of which was actually being filmed. He was a quiet ruminative pipe-smoker, not greatly communicative, but given to interjecting pithy comments into the general talk. His wife Muriel was a doctor with her own practice: greying, rather untidily dressed, practical, efficient and sympathetic.

It was Emma who, for reasons best known to herself, brought up the subject of the black dog. None of the company sitting before the glowing log fire in the great Elizabethan fireplace were greatly fond of animals, though the Berkshaws admitted to a cat. 'People who dote on animals,' said Entwistle, 'are obviously attempting to supply themselves with something they lack. One feels sorry for them, but they do tend to go and on about their benighted pets.'

'I'm thankful,' said Henry, 'we've never had a dog. A dreadful bore, having to feed and walk it, and pay for vets and kennels.'

'But darling,' said Emma, 'you've forgotten. We have got a dog.'

'Eh?' said Henry. 'Oh, surely, Emma, you don't mean...'

'We don't even have to feed him. In fact he hasn't even got a name that I know of.'

'What on earth are you talking about, Emma?' asked Muriel with a little laugh, amid general mystification.

'I'll tell you. Don't take any notice of Henry, he thinks I'm imagining things. But I've come across this dog, a black sort of Welsh collie or sheepdog, in the walled garden at the back

3

of the house, two or three times now. It seems to be looking for something, perhaps its owner. Once I actually saw it in the house, on the stairs. But each time as I get near to it, or it to me – it suddenly disappears.'

They digested this in silence, the men smiling and looking quizzically at each other. Muriel regarded Emma intently. 'Well,' she said, 'it is possible for animals, as well as humans, to leave behind them a sort of presence, a shadow or impression of themselves, when they die. And persons who are fairly psychic often come across them. I'd like to see this dog.'

'Perhaps you will,' said Emma; and the talk passed to other topics.

It was not, however, the dog that Muriel saw. To be exact, she did not *see* anything, though she heard a great deal, and sensed more. It was later that same night; a half-moon was swimming among restless clouds, dipping and soaring between them, and H.J. lay in splendid impenetrable slumber beside her as she awoke, around three o'clock, to the sound of voices close at hand. They seemed to be coming from the next room, and at first had a muffled quality; gradually they became clearer, though she could not make out the words. A man's voice, angry and threatening; a woman answering, at first in low taunting tones, then rising to a higher pitch with fear as his verbal attack mounted. Muriel, still only partly awake, lay in a half-paralysed trance-like state, listening; then came a cry of protest and pleading, ending with an agonised female scream that tore into her consciousness and shattered her bemusement, so that she leaped out of bed and went to the door.

Outside the circular landing was quiet, and a small light burning on the side of the wall showed the stair well below in shadows; the great lantern roof rose above, with the moon beyond it breasting the cumulus. The door of the room next to theirs, from whence the sounds must have come, was ajar. She pushed it open, dreading what she might find; but inside, as she saw from the moonlight and feeble glow of the lamp on the wall outside, was a single bed without a mattress or covering, a chest of drawers, and some discarded

4

Victorian paintings in elaborate gilt frames propped against the wall. The floor was bare except for a single strip of linoleum near the window. So innocent and unalarming, in fact, did the room appear, that without hesitation she actually stepped inside and tried the light switch; but it did not function, there being no bulb. She listened intently; there was no sound except for the moaning of the wind in the high beeches and the slow ominous creaking of the great cedar which then stood on the lawn in front of the house. Abruptly the temperature of the room fell, and she shivered violently; a sensation of immense and stifling malevolence assailed her, and she left the room hastily.

Outside again, she went to the door of the next room, in which she knew, Entwistle slept; she could detect from within his heavy pacific breathing, interspersed with half-snores. Returning to their own room she found H.J. still sleeping deeply. She got back into bed and lay awake for several hours, until light filtered in through the curtains, though she heard no more of the voices.

Muriel communicated this experience only to Emma. She knew that the others would only laugh and suggest various all-too plausible explanations, from dreaming to auto-suggestion; after all, they had all been discussing appari-tions only the evening before. But Muriel, who for a doctor possessed a remarkably open mind, and had read various books on psychic phenomena, was convinced that what she had heard was real enough; real in the sense that it represented something that had actually happened in the house.

She did not hear the voices again, though the next day when she and Emma ventured into the room next to hers (the men having walked to St. Meva to visit the inn) the two women underwent the identical experience Muriel had there during the night. As they stood there looking out on the trees and hearing the deep grumbling of the cedar, the room suddenly became intensely cold, and a claustrophobic atmosphere prevailed; they were subject to something powerful which drove them, shaken, out of the room: as Emma later put it, 'Something, some force, a presence, wanted to do us harm. I just had to get out.' As they went downstairs the sun lit up the lantern dome and transformed the house again into a peaceable glowing habitation. They talked over the experience and decided there was little point in discussing it with the men; the room was best left alone, so Emma decided to lock it from then on whilst they had visitors.

A black dog that disappears, screams in the night, and a room full of evil: such things can be lived with, in a large house, by intelligent unsuperstitious people, despite the unanswered questions they raise in the minds of the witnesses. But when one of the occupants is actually attacked in his bed and shows evidence of it on his person, something more positive must be done.

Ortford Entwistle had, in his younger days, been a sensitive poet, and during the late thirties had made a name for himself as a writer of trim craftsmanlike verse that actually rhymed, and dealt with matters such as unrequited love, autumn leaves, gardens in the rain, and the passing of beauty in old age. The war stopped all that sort of futile brooding, he would tell you, and after four years in the Navy (as an officer in charge of stores) he emerged in the bleak post-war years as a critical and satirical poet, abandoning rhyme and form for a wide ranging amorphous type of prose-poetry that sought to expose the vices and corruptions of society. But under his new-found carapace of cynicism there lurked still the shades of finer feelings, the old nostalgias and yearnings; perhaps, as Muriel said, if he'd found a good sensitive woman to love he wouldn't have become so ashamed of his early poetry. (Henry had all Enwistle's slim volumes, signed first editions, on his shelves). Later, on reflection, Muriel thought she could see why Ortford had been singled out for his experience. Two days after she and Emma had gone into the spare room, the poet came down to breakfast looking like a man who had met his doom but had somehow, by some default, managed to survive it.

'Good Lord... are you all right, old man?' Henry said, pausing amid a mouthful of poached egg as Entwistle appeared. Ortford stared at the company, frenetically eyed and dishevelled of hair, tieless and his collar awry, the buttons of the cardigan he wore done up on the wrong holes. He sat down and asked hoarsely for coffee. Emma poured him a cup and, after he had drunk most of it, he tried to explain, his normally reedy voice shaking, and deepened to a sandpaper huskiness.

'I don't know what time it was... towards morning, I suppose. There was still some moonlight, I think, but I was too upset to notice much. I usually sleep well, especially after a few drinks, you know; and I emphatically was not dreaming. But somehow, although asleep, I became aware, very gradually, of the feeling that something or somebody else was lying on the bed, or perhaps was actually in bed with me. I could hear this heavy slow breathing, which gradually got louder; and then I smelt a dreadful putrid odour, coming at me with each breath. Before I could collect myself sufficiently to switch on the light, this thing, whatever it was, was at me, lying on top of me, stifling me: then I felt horribly clammy cold fingers around my neck, trying to strangle me.'

'My God,' said Emma. 'What did you do?'

'By now I was fully conscious, fighting for my life, as I thought. The creature was heavy, a huge dead weight on me; but I somehow threw him, it, off, with a supreme effort, and tore myself free from the strangling grasp. It sort of slithered down in a huge heap on the floor: I got the light on then and looked down beside the bed, but there was nothing there. Then I became briefly aware, for less than a second, of a sort of brown shadow in the corner of the room. It faded immediately, and I was left alone. I was so shattered I simply got back to bed and left the light on, and lay staring at the ceiling till dawn; then I fell asleep for about an hour, and woke late for breakfast.'

'It's certainly a hell of story, or nightmare, or whatever,' said H.J., beginning to visualise it as a basis for a short story, or even a novel.

'Sure you're not getting the D.T.'s, old chap?' asked Julius Natwich. He didn't smile, because Ortford was so evidently distraught; but he could no more credit Entwistle's account as an actual event than he could believe in Atlantis or flying saucers.

Ortford looked at them all in turn, holding each of them in a terrible gaunt stare. 'If it was only a bad dream,' he said, 'can you explain this?' He loosened his collar. On each side of his windpipe was a large bruise, and, as they saw, there were further bruises at the back of his neck commensurate with the fingermarks of a heavy strangling grip. 'I can't sleep in that room any more,' he said. 'Can you put me somewhere else?'

'Of course,' Emma said. 'I'm terribly sorry you've had this experience. We'd no idea that anything like that could happen here, had we, Henry? No one told us there was anything wrong with the house.'

Henry was dumb, merely staring at his plate of gelid half-consumed egg-on-toast.

'There simply must be some rational explanation,' Julius said.

'Why?' said Muriel. 'Why does it have to be rational?'

'Because we live in a rational universe, surely.'

'Are you sure of that? In my experience there's a hell of a lot going on that's irrational. From human behaviour to natural phenomena of all sorts that we can't explain. Oh, never mind, this isn't the time or place for philosophising. Ortford's had a dreadful shock.' She turned to the distraught poet. 'Try to eat something light, and I'll give you a sedative. Lie down on the sofa in the library, and sleep for a bit.'

When Ortford, after eating some toast and drinking another cup of coffee, had retired, the others sat in the wan late December sunshine and finished their own breakfasts, animatedly discussing the event. It provided a catalyst which considerably enlivened a house party that was beginning to flag under Henry's pontifications, and the fact that the guests were running out of amusing stories and wicked observations on contemporary life and personages. Emma and Muriel now told the others of their experiences in the unused room between those slept in by the Berkshaws

8

and Entwistle. Henry was strangely subdued, listening to Natwich and H.J. trying to explain the unexplainable; suddenly he got up and said, 'I'm going into that room.'

'You'll need the key. It's on the ledge above the door,' said Emma.

'Do you want me to come with you?'

'Please yourself.' Henry mounted the stairs and went around the circular landing. The others stayed below in the hall, though Emma went up halfway and paused, listening. Henry reached the spare room, hesitated, unlocked the door and went in. A minute later, no more, he came out rather more quickly than he went in. He descended the stairs, frowning and polishing his spectacles, which had become misted over.

'Well?' said Emma.

'I see what you mean,' Henry said.

'Right,' said Emma. 'Now listen to me, please, everyone.' Her small bright bird-like face was set with decision. 'I'm going to call in Mrs. Carmichael, the medium, and ask her to go over this place. I want to know all I can about it: scoff if you like about ghosts and the supernatural, but I'm not exposing myself or anyone else to the sort of thing that happened to Ortford.'

'A medium?' said Julius. 'That's a bit much, isn't it?'

Berkshaw smiled. 'It'll be interesting to see what she makes of all this, whoever she is.'

'Who exactly is Mrs Carmichael?' Muriel wanted to know.

Emma told them. The lady, who lived a few miles away, had a reputation in the district as an eccentric, but had strong credentials among some of the villagers and farm people for having healed their various intractable complaints; in one or two cases she had described to them dead relatives of theirs whom she herself had never met. She was said to have marked clairvoyant powers, and should, Emma said, be able to help them if anyone near at hand could.

Mrs. Carmichael, it transpired, was very interested in the events which Emma had described to her over the phone. She arrived in a battered Morris Minor in time for tea, and

9

before she commenced examining the house, questioned each of them about what they had heard or seen, or believed or did not believe. Sitting there in her long tweed skirt and huge baggy cardigan, with two rows of agate beads on her large bosom, and her searching pearl-grey eyes and quiet penetrating voice, she fascinated and frightened them all into answering her accusative questions.

To Henry: 'You mean that you've lived here for four years and heard or seen nothing? You must be insensitive indeed, Professor.'

To H.J. : 'Surely as a novelist you can appreciate that an old house like this must have these associations... that over the centuries various events must have happened, to give rise to this or that phenomenon?' H.J. smiled and made a non-committal gesture, busying himself with his pipe to distract himself from those searching eyes.

To Ortford, who had recovered well enough to wonder now whether in fact what he'd experienced was real or imaginary, perhaps having been induced by the effect of the late-night whisky and roast pork he had eaten at dinner: 'Have you never undergone any occult experiences before? No poltergeistic activity, no unexplained happenings of any kind?' She seemed incredulous when Ortford, after much frowning, couldn't remember anything.

Natwich, who had sat apart with a detached and sceptical smile, was told: 'You are connected with mechanical and engineering matters. You imagine yourself safe from these happenings. But beware. I foresee a great shock coming to you; in fact, your life will be endangered.' Mrs. Carmichael had been told nothing about Julius' work or his beliefs.

She now stood up, rearranged her beads on her swaying breasts, and said, 'I'll go over the house now. I must ask this gentleman' – indicating Berkshaw – 'and this one' – Natwich – 'to stay here. They don't help my guides. I'll start in here.' She went into the library.

Emma, Muriel, Ortford and Henry accompanied her into the long room with its leather chair and booklined walls. As soon as they entered, all of them, except Henry, noticed the smell of chrysanthemums, although there were none in the room. The aroma faded as Mrs. Carmichael began her examination.

She stood in the centre of the room and closed her eyes. Her breathing became deeper and slower; she began to move with remarkably light, sure steps for a heavy person, avoiding as if by instinct every piece of furniture as she approached it. Then coming to a halt by the fireplace she spoke.

'Monks,' she muttered in a drowsy voice, her own, but in a deeper register, a tenor or baritone. 'Eating. Drinking wine. Wiping their fingers, quarrelling. One is reading from the Bible in Latin, but few listen. Atmosphere of suspicion, hatred. There is one here with a scar on his left cheek. A black dog sits beside him, he feeds it with titbits from time to time. They are eating venison and drinking freely, filling their goblets over and over. The chief of them, the Canon, speaks in a strange tongue; he is not English or Cornish. He is held in awe by the others.' She shook her head now, opened her eyes and looked at them, her normal self again. 'Most interesting. I wonder how far back all that was.'

'Before the Reformation, no doubt.' Henry was trying to be helpful.

'Do you want to see the kitchen and back rooms now?' Emma asked.

'No. Upstairs, I think.'

As they went up the staircase Mrs. Carmichael paused. 'That dog again. Does anyone else see it?'

'I do,' said Emma. 'Up there, on the top of the stair.'

'Ah.' She seemed satisfied. 'The same one you see from time to time?'

'Yes.'

They went into each of the bedrooms, leaving Ortford's until last. In each of them Mrs. Carmichael pointed out some feature which had been changed over the years: a window blocked up, a false ceiling put in, old beams concealed. Then they entered the spare room between Ortford's and the Berkshaw's bedroom. Immediately they did so Mrs. Carmichael began to shake; they could hear her necklace clattering in her agitation.

11

'Out... out!' she groaned in a strangled voice, urging them to leave with violent gestures. 'Danger. I can see him, with his sword, dripping with blood.' The room had become as cold as a mortuary. The others retreated to the doorway and watched, horrified and fascinated. 'A case of murder, surely. Yes... The other man, with the scar, the dog's owner... lying on the floor, his neck and chest bleeding. And the woman cowering in the corner. *In Nomine Patris et Filius et Spiritus Sancti*, stay away from me!'

'My God,' Ortford muttered. 'I can see...'

'What is it you can see?' asked Emma.

He shook his head. 'It's gone. But I thought I saw that shadow. And smelt that awful stench again.'

'Auto-suggestion, perhaps?' said Muriel.

'No,' Mrs. Carmichael declared, coming out of the room. 'He was right. I smelt it too. It's the Canon or his servant. They're still here, after all these years. Now for the room you slept in, Mr. Entwistle.'

She went to the door of the bedroom, opened it and looked in, but before entering made the sign of the cross over herself and the doorway. Inside all was peaceful enough in the slowly waning light. Outside the cedar creaked and groaned, though there was very little if any wind. Mrs. Carmichael looked out of the window. 'That tree. I don't like it. You ought to have it cut down before it falls.' She turned, looked around the room, closed her eyes and again breathed deeply and slowly.

'The Canon is here. Also his servant, heavy, with a dark scowling face. And an old woman.' She paused, her breathing now becoming agitated. Suddenly her body shook, and from her throat a man's voice spoke, mouthing something barely intelligible in a mixture of French, Breton and Cornish. '*Miserere, yn yffarn ov-vy. André-Robert yu ow hanow. Aidez-moi, gwra ow weres, my a'th pys... a'th pys...*' Suddenly the medium swooned to the floor. Ortford and Henry rushed to her and with some difficulty, for she weighed some twelve stones, dragged her out of the room. Muriel affirmed afterwards she was sure she heard a man's mocking laughter as they did so; but Emma thought she heard the cackling of an ancient female voice.

Mrs. Carmichael's eyes opened. Shaking, her teeth chattering and whiter than her normally pale complexion, she asked to be taken downstairs, where, after sipping a brandy, she composed herself again. 'We haven't seen it all by any means,' she said. 'A very remarkable and intriguing situation. You'll excuse me, I hope, but I can't face any more today. That evil spirit almost took over; I think you got me out just in time. But he has to be laid to rest, he and the others. May I come back again? Would the day after tomorrow be convenient?'

They were now in the week between Christmas and the New Year, the dead pause of the year, and apart from an invitation the next day to visit the Cornish Arms for a Christmas party at which the local carollers would be singing, there was no social event arranged. Henry Hawken, now thoroughly fascinated by what he had witnessed, agreed that she should return in two days time. Meanwhile, Mrs. Carmichael advised with a dark foreboding look at them all, and especially at Entwistle, that no one should go into the room Ortford had slept in, or the spare room next to it, on pain of dire but unspecified consequences.

That evening was spent in sombre speculation by hosts and guests, enlivened only by Natwich's refusal to accept Mrs. Carmichael's visions as anything other than a piece of charlatanism. He stopped only just short of becoming insulting to Emma and the Professor for entertaining such notions. 'You mean to tell me that you actually swallow this talk of evil apparitions, dripping swords, and so on? Really, Henry, I can't help being surprised.'

'I'm still at the stage of keeping an open mind, you see.' Henry said mildly. 'But after all, certain things are simply inexplicable, except in the terms Mrs. C. uses.'

'It was real enough, the experience I had,' Ortford pointed to the bruises on his throat. 'You won't convince me that was just a dream.'

'But hang it all – the whole thing's simply medieval.' Natwich regarded them with an incredulous maddening grin.

13

'Well, the house is basically medieval,' Muriel mused. 'So I suppose one must expect medieval happenings and presences.'

'And deal with them in a medieval fashion? Exorcism, and that sort of thing?' It was obviously anathema to Julius that anyone should so much as contemplate the possibility of another world beyond, or behind, or intermingled with, the physical one in which he moved.

'Now how would you deal with these things, Julius?' Emma wanted to know, fixing on him her brilliant penetrating stare. When Emma looked intently at you, there was only one possible reaction in face of such an examination. You answered as seriously and thoughtfully as you were capable of doing.

'I'm quite sure there is always a natural explanation, as distinct from a supernatural one, in these matters. Now Ortford won't have it that he dreamed that thing, but we are all subject to time-lapses and aberrations; it is quite possible to hallucinate and become terrified of what we see and feel. But such happenings are actually going on within us, rather than outside us. Surely you agree, as a doctor, Muriel?'

'Only partly,' Muriel said. 'I've never known a case where four people in a completely sober state can go into a room and register the same reaction – a sudden chill in the atmosphere and a deep sensation of evil. We all felt it: Emma and I when we first went into the spare room, and then both of us with Henry and Ortford when we went in there with Mrs. Carmichael.'

'She saw the black dog, and I'd seen it before,' Emma pointed out. 'Our descriptions of it coincide completely.'

'I'd say that was some form of thought transference.' Julius was unmoved. 'A fairly common sort of thing, it appears.'

'You mean,' Berkshaw came in here, 'that Mrs. Carmichael must have read Emma's mind? And described the dog to convince her? A bit far-fetched, surely.'

'I have an acute suspicion,' Julius told them, 'that due to some process of hallucinatory suggestions, brought on by the atmosphere of the house – it is gloomy and foreboding,

I'm not denying that – anyone who is sensitive, emotional, imaginative, is likely to create fantasies for him or herself. And then the medium comes in, tells you all sorts of highly coloured stories of what she allegedly can see, and you can't; does an effective piece of play-acting, and faints; and you swallow the lot.'

'So the screams in the night, and Ortford's assailant, were all pure imagination?' asked Henry.

Julius spread his hands non-committally. Without accusing Ortford of deliberately inducing bruises on his own throat, or Muriel of inventing the screams she had supposedly heard, he could develop his argument no further. He therefore merely smiled at Emma's invitation to spend the night in the room Ortford had vacated, and the conversation lapsed until Henry suggested a rubber or two of bridge.

The day after next brought a blustering wind and squalls of rain. H.J. and the Professor had contemplated a round of golf, but lingered on over breakfast, hoping for the weather to improve. Natwich engrossed himself in the Daily Telegraph crossword, while Ortford, who had slept reasonably well for two nights in his new room, helped Emma to clear away the dishes. Muriel, also sleeping well now (with the help of sleeping tablets), announced her intention of walking down to the cliffs, rain or shine, and went to get her raincoat.

'I'd just remind you that Mrs. C. is due here this afternoon,' Emma told them. 'If anyone is interested in what she comes up with this time, they should be back here by three o'clock. What do you propose to do, Julius?'

'I shan't be welcome when she's here, that's certain. I think I'll go down to the beach at Gwyndreath; the wreck of the Ironside is visible after the storms recently, and I'd like a close look at the bridge. It's quite old, I believe.'

A shaft of weak sunlight illuminated the grounds and the windswept bushes beyond the breakfast room. 'About 1600, the original part,' Henry said. 'Right, H.J., I think the weather's clearing a little. By the time we get on to the first tee I think we might find it quite possible.'

15

Mrs. Carmichael arrived soon after lunch. She got out of her Morris in front of the house and greeted them with a cheerful smile.

'I trust you've recovered from your experience the other day?' inquired Emma.

'Oh, certainly. Takes more than a rogue spirit to keep me down. All in a week's work, you know. Now... where shall we begin? The back court, I think, while it stays dry.'

Emma led the way through the dark passage past the former servant's quarters, through the large kitchen with its floor of slate flags, and out into the back yard, where, between the old stables and a barn were a decaying dovecote and a well, now disused and boarded over. Mrs. Carmichael, arrayed in a shabby fox-fur coat and a brilliant green scarf over her head, closed her eyes and stood still, breathing slowly. She shook her head, opened her eyes and moved around the perimeter of the yard; entered one of the stables, came out again; then, as if hypnotised, staring straight ahead of her, went to the well-cover and stood on it. She gasped and staggered, and was helped off it by Ortford and Muriel.

'I had a sudden tremendous sensation of falling... falling down the well. Wait...' She went to the cover and closed her eyes, breathing in short heavy panting gasps. 'Yes... yes... the monks again... the Canon is watching...' She placed one foot on the cover and shivered. 'They are throwing a body down the well. It's the man they killed, the dog's owner.' She opened her eyes. 'Well, we know how they disposed of the body, or hid it for a time, at any rate. Shall we go in?'

They entered the kitchen, and as they did so Muriel saw, very briefly, the black dog in the corner, pawing the floor. Presumably, she decided, the poor thing was forever searching for its dead master. But Mrs. Carmichael had stiffened, and was making the sign of the cross over herself. She closed her eyes. They paused and stared at her. 'The Canon... is here. He is trying to tell... to tell me...' A silence, during which she did not breathe at all; then a man's voice said from her throat, 'Aidez-moi. Gwer dhym. Aidez, s'il vous plait. Ny allaf merwel. Je veux mourir. Mea culpa. Aidez-moi, je vous en prie'.

Emboldened to act before the medium got into further difficulties, Emma asked in firm ringing tones, 'How can we help you? You are dead. We are from another age, five or six hundred years in the future. You have been dead all this while. *Mort, vous êtes vraiment mort. Comprenez-vous?*'

The voice sighed and groaned, and said, '*Si je suis mort, pourquoi n'ai-je pas le repos? Yn yffarn my yu. En enfer, mes yeyn yu, il n'est pas chaud ici.*'

Muriel said, taking over from Emma, 'Confess. Ask forgiveness for your misdeeds. *Faîtes-vous confession. Priez pour absolution.*'

More groans. Mrs. Carmichael's face was expressionless, her lips unmoving; she stood there rigidly, her eyes fast closed. A consummately clever ventriloquist's act, Ortford thought, if this is a hoax.

'I will try to,' the Canon's voice said. '*Je ferai confession pour mes péchés.* Aaaah...' They thought the medium was going to swoon again; she wavered, but recovered her balance as Emma reached out to steady her.

'*Méchant nous sommes tous. Oll ny yu peghadoryon... damnés, damnés!*'

'How many of you are there?' Muriel wanted to know.

'*Douze. Deudhek.* And the woman. *Ow benen. La vielle aussi. Pêcheurs tous, tous. Nous avons tué. Ladha ny a wruk.*'

Emma was signing the cross over Mrs. Carmichael, when there came a quake which shook the whole house, rattling crockery and knocking pictures askew on the walls; followed by a man's terrified yell from outside. 'My God...' Muriel ran up the passage followed by Ortford. Emma, left alone with the medium, heard a low wicked chuckle come from her throat; she could not decide whether it was the Canon's voice, or another.

Julius Natwich had, as planned, set off in his raincoat and walking boots down to the beach, which he had reached after twenty minutes. He had spent half an hour poking about there examining the ironwork of the wreck sunken in the sands (she was a large merchant vessel which had grounded here in the 1920s and broken up on the rocks, becoming gradually swallowed up, though from time to time parts of her gunwales and bows became visible.) Then he had gone back to the humpbacked bridge and, having examined that and checked the date chiselled into a granite stone in its parapet coping (1623), he had seen more large squally clouds approaching, and decided to walk smartly back to Roskilly House. The clouds passed by with a mere scatter of rain; on reaching the gates and seeing Mrs. Carmichael's vehicle before the house, he had undertaken a small perambulation around the grounds rather than go inside just yet.

At this point the wind was dropping rather than rising. When he had traversed the paths branching out from either side of the gravel drive, among laurels, rhododendrons and camelias in their sober winter glossiness, he resolved that he would, after all, go in, medium or no medium; but as he drew level with the great cedar on the lawn, conscious of its huge branches with their leaves in horizontal swathes, he became aware of a series of querulous tortured complaints in the upper part of the bole; these developed into a splitting groan and, looking up he saw that one side of the massive tree, the side under which he was now walking, was tearing away from the main trunk and was in the process of falling. The mass of heavy branches covered in dark green needles, looming down upon him to crush him utterly, was a split-second sight that was to remain with him for the rest of his life. But terrified as he was he did not hesitate; he ran, back the way he had come, and if he had not stumbled he might have got free. As it was, one of the longer lower branches caught him across the back as it came down, sending him sprawling forward on to his stomach, whilst a secondary bough pinned him down, fracturing his leg.

They had to fetch a saw to free him. Henry and H.J. returned from their golf in time to help carry him inside, and Muriel ministered to him, giving him hot tea and aspirins, advising that he should be taken immediately to the casualty department of the Royal Cornwall Infirmary at Truro. She and H.J. decided to drive him down themselves.

Meanwhile Mrs. Carmichael had sat, withdrawn and shaken, apart from them all in the corner of the library. After the Berkshaws had driven off with Julius she called a conference.

'I hope,' she said in a low deep voice, 'that after what happened this afternoon none of you will doubt me when I say that this house is subject to malign influences, the heritage of past evil which lives on. My spirit guides warn me not to set foot inside the place again, unless you undertake to accept their directions.'

'What directions, Mrs. C.?' asked Henry.

'We must take action to neutralise the influences. Nullify them. Lay them to rest.'

'Exorcism?' said Ortford.

Mrs. Carmichael fixed upon them her sepulchral gaze. 'No; not that. We must not be so medieval. For even evil spirits can repent and be forgiven. That is what they must be persuaded to do, and we must help them.'

'But how?' asked Emma.

'I have a clergyman friend, well versed in these matters, who will come and hold a service here: a cleansing, an exhortation to repent, confess, receive absolution. Exorcism, you see, merely curses and banishes these agents elsewhere, so although they cause no more trouble here, they go on in torment elsewhere. Would you agree to what I propose?'

Henry said, speaking for all, 'I'm sure we would be pleased to try anything. I take it that you believe the tree falling wasn't an accident?'

'I had a distinct vision... a telepathic view... of those influences at work on the tree.'

'Well, I've heard of tables moving, and even heavy furniture, but a huge tree like that...' Emma's credulity was being strained.

'It was, after all, fairly old,' Henry reflected. 'About seventy or eighty years old, I believe. These conifers are subject to frost getting in their joints, I'm told...'

'I am utterly certain of what happened.' Mrs. Carmichael would have no arguments. 'The wind was dropping, not rising, when it happened.'

'True,' Henry said, recalling the easing of the blustery

19

squalls with which he and H.J. had battled for almost eighteen holes.

'Mrs. Carmichael's right,' said Ortford. 'It was no coincidence that it fell on Julius, the worst sceptic of us all.'

'Very well, Mrs. C.' Emma was firm. 'Please ask your reverend friend to come. I feel we must see this through.'

Not only for themselves, she felt; for those restless tortured spirits, agencies, poltergeists, whatever one chose to call them. For it was clear enough to her that they were entities which cried out through their very actions and ominous presences that they needed help. She wondered whether Julius would revise his attitude to them now.

So it was arranged that the following Sunday afternoon the Revd. Claude Slogget would come and hold his service at Roskilly House. Mrs. Carmichael departed, driving her car over the lawn to skirt the fallen tree.

The happenings of that day, Wednesday, produced a distinct change in Julius, who, his leg now in plaster, was brought back the following day to move awkwardly about on crutches or rest with his leg up on the sofa. He was withdrawn, pale, highly annoyed but quiescent; he did not wish to discuss the tree or what the others had seen or felt, though he listened without his previous superciliousness when they discussed them in his hearing. For the most part he consoled himself with detective stories, the *Encyclopaedia Britannica*, and crosswords. And when Sunday came he insisted on being present at the service.

The Revd. Slogget was a small round-faced man with spectacles and a rich imposing baritone voice. He listened gravely to what they all had to recount, and Mrs. Carmichael, whom he called Gladys, was asked to give her explanation of the events as far as it had been made known to her by the guides and her own intuition.

'The house,' said Mrs. Carmichael in hushed tones, 'was an appurtenance of the monastery at Bodmin until the Dissolution. Being isolated and near the coast, a good many strange and violent happenings evidently occurred here; the worst of which seems to be the killing by the Canon of the scar-faced monk, a matter of jealousy over the woman they kept for their pleasure – in the spare room between the Berkshaws' and Ortford's former bedroom. The old crone whom I have described seems to be very much at enmity with the mistress, as if blaming her for causing trouble among the monks. I haven't been able to identify the malignant force which attacked Mr. Entwistle, but I would guess it is the heavy dark servant of the Canon, whom I saw with his master in the room where Mr. Entwistle slept previously. All these spirits, having connived at the murder, presumably because the scar-faced monk had been having an affair with the Canon's mistress, have become so confirmed in their evil doings that they remain here long after their physical bodies are dead, reliving their terrible acts. But the Canon at least appears to be aware that he has done wrong, and yearns for release. Which is why, Reverend Slogget, we have asked you here.'

'Thank you, Gladys. Now, Mrs. Hawken, we will begin. Where would you suggest we summon these unhappy beings?'

'Here in the library, I think; do you agree, Mrs. Carmichael?'

The medium nodded. 'They were all gathered here, which was their refectory, including the scar-faced monk and the dog. Yes. Will you begin, Mr. Slogget?'

'I want you all to kneel and pray. Even if you are an agnostic, please try to attune yourself in sympathy with our efforts to intercede for these wretched ones. They are living on in their own hell, and we are going to try to obtain their release.' Julius, his legs up on the sofa, put down his newspaper and, Emma noted out of the corner of her gaze, closed his eyes, frowning as if in supplication as the others knelt.

'Almighty Father, who in Thine eternal mercy wilt forgive each one of us who doth repent and turn to Thee at the last, whatever the weight of his sins and wrongdoings, hear our prayer, that this house may be hallowed anew and dedicated to Thee, that all restless and tortured spirits shall be absolved, and all forces of evil henceforth be banished. We trust in Thine everlasting compassion that these our

21

earthbound brothers and sisters may finally obtain peace and rest in Thine arms. Amen.'

'Amen,' they all dutifully repeated; even Julius' lips moved.

At a nod from the priest Mrs. Carmichael stood in the centre of the room, closed her eyes and went into her trance induction: breathing slowly and heavily, until, her lips soundlessly moving, there issued unintelligible words, a man's voice mumbling from her unmoving throat.

'Who is here?' asked the priest, in commanding forthright tones. 'Speak: we are here to help you.'

After more muttering, the words, 'Canon André-Robert,' were heard, among unrecognisable sounds, and an old woman's chuckle.

'You have killed a man, is it not so?'

'*J'ai tué.* I have killed, *yn wyr.*'

'Do you repent and ask forgiveness?'

'*Mais oui.* I do. I do.'

'Is there more you would confess?'

'*Hep dowt.* Fornication. Jealousy, drunkenness; I have kept back monies from the monastery. Lies and deceit, my days were full of them. *Pardonnez-moi, A Dhew a'n ughella. Laissez-moi reposer!*'

As the Canon's foreign voice, with its strange mixture of languages, came through, Henry Hawken was amazed and fascinated to visualise the sort of man who was confessing: vividly and without effort, he saw him, large, thick-set and bearded, nearing sixty, his face troubled, the anxiety superimposed upon the floridity of years of good living: in every seam and fold of flesh sensuality and indulgence were written, in the rich lips and the proud curl of the nostrils, the aristocratically curved nose and heavy dark eyebrows, the pouches under the shrewd avaricious eyes. Afterwards Henry came to believe he had actually seen André-Robert as he had existed in life, that it had been no imaginary impression.

'Sin no more,' intoned the Revd. Slogget. 'You have served your penance all these dark years. *In nomine Patris et Filius et*

Spiritus Sancti, ego te absolvat. Depart in peace, to thy eternal rest. Amen.'

Silence.

'Is anyone else here? Speak and we will help.'

A woman's voice this time, weeping, but gradually evolving into speech. 'I am here. Yselt Constance.'

'Who are you, Yselt? Are you the Canon's paramour?'

'I am. For years I was his mistress, until Myghal Jehane came here to be steward. He loved me, I loved him. I could not give myself to the Canon after that. So André-Robert killed him...' More weeping. 'I have suffered great grief all this time.'

As these words were spoken Ortford had a sudden brief vision of a distraught woman: aged perhaps twenty-eight or thirty, with long black hair, a pale face and large weeping grey-green eyes, full lips and a delicate long nose; she wore a flowing dress with a bodice laced over her breast, and long full sleeves. This image of her was to remain with him for many years.

'And remorse?' pursued the priest. 'Do you repent of your sins?'

'Yes, yes, I repent. I have been lustful and impure. I am ashamed. Help me!'

'*In nomine Patris et Filius...*'

One by one the dead announced themselves, were urged to name and repent of their evil deeds, and were granted absolution. At last, after the twelfth monk had spoken and been granted his release, a shrill cackling female voice was heard.

'Who is this? What is your name?'

'Old Isabel, the housekeeper.' A cracked, witch-like snigger. 'Once I was the Canon's mistress, before he took on that young hussy Yselt... I saw what went on here for many years. May she rot in Hell! The harlot carried on with more than one before *he* came, Jehane, the man they murdered.'

'Answer, Isabel: do you wish to confess your sins? Or do you want to remain here alone in this limbo, this hell on earth?'

23

A pause, followed by a feline snarl. 'Very well. I will confess. To adultery, to envy, malice and hatred.'

'And do you truly repent of those things, and love your enemies; even Yselt?'

'I do... repent.' The words came with difficulty, like teeth being drawn, as though a residue of evil and resentment remained. The Revd. Slogget said firmly, 'Without absolution you cannot find rest. Isabel, forgive your enemies, if such they truly were. Swear never to harm them again.'

'Very well, I swear. Mary, Mother of God, give me rest. Jesus, dear Christ, forgive me these years of sin.' The voice was becoming faint, a whimpering whisper now, but it carried conviction.

'*In Nomine Patris et Filius et Spiritus Sancti...*' Old Isabel was given absolution, and was silent. The medium stood swaying slightly, her breathing coming in slow deep laboured spasms now.

'Is there anyone else left in this house who requires rest and forgiveness?'

From the throat of Mrs. Carmichael came a whining, then a short plaintive bark. 'The black dog,' whispered Emma. 'We mustn't forget the dog. And what about his master?'

'Myghal Jehane,' said the priest in thunderous abjuration, his voice ringing through the house. 'Where is Myghal Jehane, whom the dog seeks?'

A pause whilst they all listened, and only the spasmodic half-snoring breaths of the medium could be heard; then a voice as cold as the grave said haltingly, 'Here I am. The man the Canon killed and buried beneath the floorslabs of your kitchen, after they had thrown my body down the well to conceal it from the Prior on his Visitation. I have lain there for five hundred years or more, in a limbo of cold clay, while my tormentors held the house over me.'

'Confess and ask forgiveness, Myghal, and you shall attain rest at last.' A whine and a scuffling noise. 'And your faithful hound as well.'

So Jehane confessed and was absolved, and the spirits were all laid to rest, even the dog. The Revd. Slogget went to Mrs. Carmichael, took her by the hand, and gently stroked it. 'All over, Gladys. Our work is done,' he murmured. The medium's eyes opened, her body relaxed, and he led her to an armchair into which she sank. After a few moments her breathing became lighter, easier, regaining its normal rhythm. Then she opened her eyes. 'Well, there!' she said brightly. 'I could do with a good hot cup of tea. Is there one going?'

These events each in their own way produced lasting effects on the witnesses to them. Julius Natwich never again questioned or criticised the evidence of paranormal happenings, though for the rest of his life he avoided all discussion and involvement with them.

H.J. Berkshaw pondered long over what he had seen and heard, and the idea of writing a story or a novel about them pursued him for many years; but he could never quite decide whether it ought to be a straight horror tale, or a satirical black comedy. He did, however, develop an obsessive taste for occult films and works of fiction.

Ortford Entwistle could not forget the face of Yselt; she came in time to dominate his consciousness so much that he wrote three long serious poems about her and her times. They won him the Eliot Memorial Prize for poetry, and when published, set him on a new career, reviving and enlarging what he saw as his true and original style.

Muriel was sufficiently impressed by Gladys Carmichael's mediumship to examine other activities of hers, including the spirit healing she practised; she referred to her certain cases of extreme difficulty among her patients, including some of terminal cancer and leukaemia, with beneficial and (in one or two instances) startling results.

Emma and Henry Hawken lived on in Roskilly House for three years after these events, and had no further abnormal experiences. Not even the black dog was seen again, and once, greatly daring, Emma spent the night in the room in which Entwistle had first slept, with no ill effects. Even when she went into the spare room next to it she could detect nothing unusual; though looking out of the window on to the lawn and massive stump of the cedar tree which had so nearly crushed Julius, she could not suppress a shudder at the memory of that event.

Ten years after they moved, the house was bought for an hotel; extensions were made to the back of it, during the course of which the kitchen floor slabs were removed. Beneath them the skull and bones of a man were found, dated by the local pathologist at about 1450 A.D.

Meanwhile Professor Hawken had acquired a new subject, which he now studied with immense dedication; he read and researched all he could into paranormal occurrences, telepathy, psychokinesis, poltergeistic phenomena and related themes. He joined the Society for Psychic Research and became a leading figure in its activities; his monograph, 'In Defence of Paranormality,' was widely acclaimed, and he began a treatise on Intellectual Aspects of Extra-Sensory Perception; though sadly he did not live to complete it. But his lectures to various societies became quite a vogue, being generally agreed to be most lively and interesting, before he himself passed over to what he called the Other Side.

THE HERETIC

At times one has, for reasons not at all obvious, the most shattering and amazingly vivid dreams which stand out in every detail, and which, despite the passing of time, remain engraved on one's memory. This last alone makes them remarkable, for of the many thousands of dreams we may dream during our lives, the vast majority are, of course, recountabie only in a brief hazy manner; we are left with mere ephemeral waking impressions that usually vanish utterly when we attire ourselves and go about our business.

One outstanding dream which I had – and even now, more than twenty years later, I cannot utterly convince myself that it *was* a dream, that it was not, in fact, an actual experience – took place on a visit to Exeter. I was then a commercial traveller representing a well-known firm making knitwear, and I came to the city regularly three or four times a year to sell to the shops. Normally I stayed at the Rougemont Hotel, in the centre of the old town, where many of my travelling friends also gathered; after dinner we usually enjoyed a round or two of drinks in the comfortable bar, and talked shop, or sport, or passed on the latest risqué jokes. But on that particular occasion, during the autumn, the hotel was closed for alterations and I had to find other accommodation. I was advised to try the White Hart, an old establishment a few streets away outside the medieval city wall.

I found a place to park at the rear of the inn, in what had evidently been the stable yard in the old days of coaching, and went in. I was immediately interested by the place. It had a dark, slightly decrepit but mysterious atmosphere; I like old buildings, and delight at probing into their histories. The establishment proudly claimed to date from the seventeenth century.

I found the landlord, who scratched his head when I asked for a room, and said he was full up. His wife, who came to the little reception office as I was inquiring,

27

murmured something about Number Twelve. The landlord shrugged, and said, 'We do actually have a spare room; it hasn't any central heating, but we can make up a bed there if you'll give us half an hour.' I nodded, and he said to his wife, 'Ask them to light a fire there, will you?'

So I signed in, glad to be relieved of further search for lodging, and went into the bar. There was no dining room, but they provided me with a decent basket of fried chicken and chips, and after a couple of pints of their best bitter I felt distinctly drowsy. I'd had a long day motoring down from south London (the motorway had not then reached Exeter), and had made several calls on the way, bringing in my samples of pullovers, cardigans and other garments in heavy cases each time. I listened for a moment or two to the talk in the bar, but was not inclined to stay; I had some orders to write out, and decided to go up to my room.

They had taken my case up for me, I found, and on inquiring for a key was told that the maid was up there and would let me in. 'Up the second flight of stairs, and turn left, sir,' the landlord said. 'Number Twelve is right at the end. The bathroom's down on the first floor – I hope you don't mind. Watch your head as you go up.'

The ancient boards of the inn creaked, and the stairway ceiling was indeed so low that a tall person would have had difficulty in negotiating it safely. The black beams in the wall were set at strange angles, and the wainscotting bulged and buckled. 'Seventeenth century seems right,' I thought as I picked my way along up to the second floor. Halfway along the short dark passage I noticed a modern number '12' on a door, and stopped. I tried the handle, but it was locked. Puzzled, I stepped back, and then was addressed by a young woman's voice to my right. She had emerged from the room at the end. 'Number Twelve, Sir, this way.'

She ushered me into a small low-ceilinged room smelling faintly of must or mildew. However, a fire blazed cheerfully in the grate, and the air was warm enough. 'I've aired the sheets and put two hot-water bottles in for you,' she said in a pleasant westcountry voice.

'Funny, having two Number Twelves,' I remarked. 'To

avoid a Thirteen, I suppose.'

'I expect so, sir. Will you have tea or coffee brought in the morning?'

I ordered tea at seven-thirty.

'Will there be anything else?' she asked.

'No. No, thank you.'

'Your key's on the dressing table.'

It was indeed: a large antiquated, half-rusty thing. I stood staring at it, and when I turned she was gone. In the low light of the flickering fire I hadn't taken much notice of her, but I had an impression of a finely chiselled face, dark hair and large luminous grey eyes. I parted the curtains drawn across the one small window, and looked down on the stable yard; I could just see the corner of my car to one side. A fine drizzle was glistening on the roof-tiles below in the lamplight. I turned to the fire and poked at it, causing it to blaze up more brightly, took out my pyjamas and hung up my travelling clothes. Then, finding a convenient chair at the dressing-table, I sat down to write out my orders. A murmur of voices along the passage, and the opening and closing of doors, told me that other people were coming to bed early.

An hour later I was in bed myself. The mattress was a soft feather tie (I was surprised that such things still existed), and I sank down into its billowy folds gratefully, the hot-water bottles sliding down on me as I did. Within seconds I was asleep.

It was the deep stupor of semi-exhaustion which often accompanies travelling, and I have come to regard it as one of the quiet pleasures of life, to end the day on the road thus. I do, however, resent being woken out of it after only an hour or two, and in my semi-consciousness fought against the very real screaming I could hear. But it was a woman's cry, and I am sufficiently gallant or old-fashioned to react to females in distress. As the sound continued I sat up in bed, listening intently.

It came from outside, down in the courtyard, I thought, as I got out of bed. The embers of the fire still glowed in the grate; the time was probably not long past midnight. I thrust back the curtains. There below I saw horses, and men in breeches carrying straw and bundles of faggots. A young woman in a shawl and long dress was pursuing a large ungainly man, who was attired in a doublet, riding boots and soft black cap with a feather; she was dragging at his elbow as he marched here and there, issuing orders. Roughly he pushed her aside, and she continued to scream out what sounded now to me to be terrified entreaties.

Hardly stopping to wonder why those people were there, and dressed in such a manner, I pulled on the light dressing-gown I take with me on my journeys, and went out. The passageway on the second floor was not lit, but a low light came from the landing below. I managed to get down to the ground floor, and looked about for a door which would lead to the landlord's private quarters. I found at the end of the passageway behind the bar such a door, marked 'Private'; tried the handle, and went in. There was silence beyond it, and darkness. 'Hullo – is anyone awake?' I called. No answer; nothing stirred. 'Hullo!' I called, louder. 'Landlord! Is anyone there?'

And then I heard that screaming again, even more urgently begging and pleading than before, as if someone threatened with terrible torture or death were imploring mercy. Lights now showed from outside in the yard, and the sound of cartwheels, scores of feet trampling, and a surging mutter of voices came to me. The light showed me the back door of the Inn, and I could not prevent myself going to it, unlocking it and drawing back the bolts at the top and bottom.

I opened the door and witnessed a commotion and a gathering such as I never beheld before or since. The approaching crowd was in high spirits, shouting and laughing and pushing a cart on which stood a middle-aged woman in a simple white smock, uncommonly like a shroud; which, I realised a little later, it actually was. A pile of faggots had been built up over a mound, and a long stake driven into the turf stood up among them. The young dark-haired woman who had been pleading with the man now ran into the crowd, trying to reach the shrouded woman in the cart: her voice was momentarily drowned in the uproar, many of the people, both men and women, evidently being full of ale and intent on making a great spectacle for themselves to enjoy. Then I lost sight of the young woman, though later I saw her on the ground, half-trampled. But I could only watch the crowd and the woman in white, up there on the cart, her hands bound before her gripping the rail.

She was a stoutish short person, with wild unkempt greying hair: no magnificent personage this; yet her eyes were uplifted and glowed out with a triumph that scorned the rabble about her. She seemed to be looking over the heads of the crowd, beyond the mound of faggots and the stake, to the deeps of heaven itself. I wanted to step forward, to try to halt the awful jollity and obscene anticipation of the crowd, but stood there transfixed, unable to cry out or move. The crowd finally halted before the mound, and the man who had been organising the pyre came forward with another person: the latter resplendent in red cloak, black broad-brimmed hat, and a chain of office around his neck. I took him for a judge, constable, or perhaps the Mayor of the city.

This gentleman held a scroll of paper or parchment in one hand, and a long staff of office in the other. Seeing him the crown swiftly hushed, and held their breaths in expectation. Behind the great man stood two figures in black trunks and doublets, their faces masked, holding aloft torches that flared and fumed into the night.

'Agnes Prest, you have been tried and convicted of heresy, and have been condemned to be burned to death at this stake unless you recant. The Queen in her majesty is merciful to those who turn back to the true Catholic faith. This last chance is given you, and your husband and children plead with you to take it and be restored to them.' At this point the girl who had been left on the ground by the surging mob raised an arm and cried out piteously something that sounded, though I could not be sure, like the word 'Murder!' 'How say you, Agnes Prest, will you still condemn yourself to the flames, or do you truly repent and recant of your heresies?'

The woman on the cart slowly brought her gaze down to look calmly at the Mayor, the executioners, the hushed crowd at her feet, and at the wan figure lying the ground. Her voice rose clear and impassioned, slightly hoarse, but rising to a kind of ecstasy. 'I believe in the Protestant Faith, and accept no Popery, nor mass nor idolatry. Before this night is out I shall see my heavenly spouse Lord Jesus Christ in glory... You slaves of Rome who rant and roar here will see me in heaven while you burn in Hell!...'

But the rabble would hear no more of this, and roared out, vilifying her: mud was thrown, splattering the white shroud, and a stone struck her on the shoulder. She bore this proudly, smiling at them all. Through the execrations I saw the Mayor gesturing to the dark figures for her execution. So she was brought down from the cart and tied to the stake; the crowd withdrew to leave a space around the piled faggots and brushwood. The woman's eyes closed and her lips moved in prayer. 'I forgive you all for this thing you do, without knowing what it is...' I heard her say; yet I know I could not have heard her voice above the mutterings and curses of the spectators swirling about her, for she was then too far away for her voice to carry to me.

The torches plunged into the tinder-wood, and flames shot up, crackling and exploding; the woodsmoke eddied and rushed around the martyred woman, whose face and eyes, transfigured, seemed to be fixed on the skies as if she could indeed see her Saviour descending to claim her soul. But the roaring of the flames increased, and at the last she shrieked out with a soul-shaking terrible agony that I still hear after all these years, as clearly as if it had only been yesterday; and expired. Even the mob, at this, fell temporarily silent, as if they too dimly realised that this woman had, in dying for her faith, somehow triumphed over them. But then the ranting and obscene jubilation broke out again as they chanted, 'The witch is dead, to hell with her, the witch is dead...'

Sickened by the scene, and my frustration and sorrow at not being about to help or intervene, I turned back to the door of the inn and went inside.

A knocking at the door awakened me. 'Your tea, sir. Good morning.'

It was the same chambermaid; she drew back the curtains and placed the tea on the cabinet beside the bed. In the weak rain-washed light of the morning my eyes opened on the long dark hair, the delicately shaped face, and I suddenly sat up, staring at her. It was the same face and form I had seen screaming and pleading with the man in charge.

'Anything wrong, sir?' she inquired.

'No... not wrong.' I groped for words, which didn't come easily after my disturbed sleep. 'Are you local?'

'Oh yes.' She smiled. 'My family's been in Exeter and Devon for centuries. My uncle traced our family tree back to fourteen hundred and something. In fact one of my ancestors was burnt as a heretic, right here outside the old city walls.'

I stared at her, then apologised for doing so. 'What's your name, may I ask?'

'Prest, sir. It goes back to Agnes Prest, the one who was burnt, and before. In fact my middle name is Agnes, in memory of her. I'm Mary Agnes, you see.'

'Ah,' I said. 'That's interesting.' But I couldn't piece it all together at that moment. 'Thank you, Mary. I had this strange dream last night...' And told her about it. But even as I recounted it all the whole thing remained so vivid and compelling before my mind's eye that I could hardly believe it had only been a dream; maybe, I thought, I've been through some time-slip and got back to the sixteenth century. (I reflected afterwards that there had been no cars in the courtyard, nor any impression of streetlamps outside. It had certainly been no mere masquerade that I had witnessed). Mary Agnes listened wide-eyed, then said, 'I've got an idea that other people have had that sort of dream here. Perhaps that's why the room isn't used much. I haven't worked here long, so I don't know. You could ask the landlord.'

And, at breakfast time, I did ask. The landlord was not about, but his wife listened to my tale, nodded sympathetically and said. 'To tell you the truth, when we took over the place four years ago we were warned that the room you're in was haunted. The previous people said somebody had had a bad experience there. I'm not superstitious, but I did feel there was a funny sort of atmosphere there. As it's small and only takes a single person we just use it as an extra, and store stuff there sometimes. I'm sorry if you were disturbed... If you want to stay another night I could move you. We've got one or two other rooms available now.'

I did wish to stay another night, to complete my business, but on reflection decided not to move. I slept in the same room, wondering, even in a queer way hoping, that the experience would be repeated. But I slept long and dreamlessly, and found out no more at that particular time to explain the occurrence.

☆☆☆

It was more than a year later when, on another trip to Exeter, I called on a good customer to find he was away ill, and could do no business. It was then early afternoon. Having no more appointments until the following day, I wandered into the City Library and Museum.

During the course of my browsing there I came across Foxe's *Book of Martyrs*, in an eighteenth century edition illustrated with vivid if somewhat crude woodcuts, and found an account there of poor Agnes Prest. Later I read other accounts, one of them in Dr A.L. Rowse's *Tudor Cornwall*; and the story began to piece itself together, corresponding at important points to what I had experienced at the White Hart Inn.

It was in the reign of the boy king, Edward VI, on the introduction of the English Prayer Book and sermons against the Pope and Catholic rites, that Agnes Prest, of Boyton on the border between Cornwall and Devon, became a fervent convert to the new faith. She could neither write nor read, but she had a formidable memory and could soon quote long passages of scripture. Like many an argumentative lay person, uneducated but with a mind used to absorbing knowledge, she could bring forth opinions and evidence persuasive to those less well-versed in such matters. The prelates and doctors who knew more could see well enough the flaws and misconceptions in her talk, but could do little to correct them. Persons like Agnes are set in their way, and argue from what they consider proven ground – in Agnes' case she had had a Vision or Experience, which caused her resolutely to proclaim and pursue her beliefs. When Edward died and his Catholic sister Mary came to the throne, Agnes, like many, was arraigned before her Bishop and Chancellor.

Bishop Turberville of Exeter wanted no trouble. He examined Agnes, who had left her husband and children, all devout Catholics, and was earning her living by spinning. He did not consider her railings against the Mass and idols to be of much account, nor did Chancellor Blackstone, who was in fact rather amused by them. 'My lord,' said the latter, ''tis plain that this woman is but a poor mazed creature, and can do little harm. Who will take her babble seriously?'

They set her at liberty, but lodged her with the keeper of the Bishop's prison, so that they could keep an eye on her. Agnes, to whom her heavenly Spouse was more important than her fleshly husband, set to spinning and carding wool and selling it in the market.

According to Foxe, she was 'as simple a woman to see as any might behold: of very little and short stature, somewhat thick, about fifty-four years of age. She had a cheerful countenance, so lively, as though she had been prepared for that day of her marriage to meet the Lamb: most patient in her words and answers, sober in apparel, meat and drink, and would never be idle: a great comfort to as many would talk with her: good to the poor; and in her trouble, money, she said, she would take none; for, she said, "I am going to a city where money beareth no mastery; whilst I am here, God hath promised to feed me." '

It seems a trifle too idealistic a portrait. Going about the city Agnes would too often get into theological disputes and arguments. She would denounce the doctrine that the bread and wine of the Mass were actually Christ's flesh and blood.

Once in the cathedral she found a German sculptor repairing images disfigured a few years before in Edward's reign, and railed against him for beautifying idols. Enraged, the sculptor turned on her and called her a whore; which led almost to a brawl, and Agnes was ejected from the church.

The Bishop and other church officials tried to get her to return to her family, but she was determined to go on preaching her version of the truth. Chancellor Blackstone would send for her, ostensibly for this purpose, but in reality to divert himself and his mistress as they dined. At last, becoming a nuisance in the streets with her disputations, she was brought to the Guildhall, charged with heresy and convicted; and handed over to the Mayor and Justices for execution. Again and again they exhorted her to recant, obtain her liberty and return to her husband and children. But Agnes was firmly set upon martyrdom, and in November 1558 she was burned at Southernhay just outside the city walls.

Thus the pathetic vision of this half-mad, saintly woman will remain with me to the last. As I think of her I seem to see that tortured age, the whole seething confusion of religious conflicts and loyalties, dividing families against themselves, son against father, wife against husband. On both sides people died bravely for their faiths, by burning, and by hanging, drawing and quartering, their entrails torn out of their still living bodies; or by rotting to death in pestilent prisons. Latimer, Ridley and Cranmer were martyred in Mary's reign; when Elizabeth succeeded the Catholic priests and recusants were persecuted, and among others Cuthbert Mayne was horribly executed at Launceston. It was an era of torment and triumph, disaster and glory. And it is in the glory of the flames by which she chose to go to her heavenly Spouse that I see Agnes Prest, praying for herself and her executors outside the walls of Exeter. Also that dark-haired girl, screaming for mercy, her face that of the young chambermaid who attended me: crying out not, as I had thought in my dream or translated experience, 'Murder' – but 'Mother!'

THE FARMER'S WIFE

One March weekend in the year 1872 a young school teacher was tramping the hills and valleys between Devon and Somerset, searching for the Doone Valley.

Hugh Varney was a great reader, and having become fascinated by the novel *Lorna Doone*, had left his lodgings in Exeter, taken the train to Barnstaple and the horse omnibus as far as Blackmore Gate; and now, walking down the lanes among mossy hedges tipped by spikes of furze, he was on Exmoor.

At that time Badgworthy Water had not been nationally proclaimed as the site of the Doone Valley (the novelist himself was reticent on the point); but using his natural intelligence and a recently published edition of the Ordnance Survey map of the area, Hugh, plodding systematically up that dramatic stream among staring sheep and goats, satisfied himself that here, at least, was a scene that answered to most of the features described in the story. Here indeed big John Ridd could have come, from his farm on the borders of the two counties, to spy on the infamous brigands and fall in love with the delightful jet-haired Lorna.

The Saturday on which he set out was fine, though very cold, with a stiff north-east wind penetrating the heather and bracken-covered fastnesses. He had walked to Oare church from Brendon, had seen the place where Lorna had been shot through the window by Carver Doone, then gone along the narrow lanes below the steep hillsides to Malmsmead, to explore the valley beside the Water. The wind grew stronger, boring into his back despite his thick serge overcoat; he wore a tweed deerstalker hat with flaps that let down to cover one's ears, which he was now glad to do.

About mid-afternoon he found the dry valley which joins the Badgworthy from the west, and was intrigued by its features; he could well believe that a century or more previously a robber band had lived here, raiding various farms on the Moor with impunity. He even found remains of cottages or huts, which might have been shepherds' shelters, or, as he thought, the vestiges of a small village as described in the novel.

He now rested on a dry outcrop of rock and listened to the wind softly wooing and whistling in the scrub oaks and rowan trees; the ever-musical tumbling of the Badgworthy stream came to him with it. Where, he wondered, was the great slide of water up which Jan Ridd had climbed to find the hideout of the Doones?

The sky darkened, threatening snow. He had planned to get back to Brendon to lodge at the inn there for the night; it was time to retrace his steps in case a blizzard should descend. No more exploring until another time, he decided with some regret. Yet, happy in his discovery, he moved briskly back the way he had come, under the branches of gnarled hawthorns and slender ash trees, beside the icy torrent spouting and gushing over time-worn granite stones. As he saw the lights of cottages at Malmsmead the snow began to fall, and by the time he had tramped over the bridge at the tiny hamlet and gone half a mile up the lane towards Brendon the roads were white and his boots wet with it. Brendon was two miles off; the hour was about five, and he had not eaten since breakfast apart from a cup of milk and slice of bread he had had at a dairy at Malmsmead on reaching it at noon. Just then he heard the sound of approaching hooves, muffled by the snow, and a thickset rubicund man with side-whiskers, driving a dog cart, came round the bend. He pulled on the reins to slow his pony as he saw Hugh.

'Whoa,' he said, stopping the animal. 'Evening, young man. And where be going, if I may ask?'

'To Brendon, sir,' said Hugh. 'I shall put up at the inn there.'

'You'll find it hard going. There's already a gurt drift of snow on the hill back there, and plenty more falling. I'm going down here to Porton farm, I be, to my cousin Samuel's wedding feast; he got married at Oare church this afternoon; I've just been home to milk my cows, y'know. But why don't yew come 'long wi' me? Sam'l an' his new wife'll be plaised to see yew, and you'll have some lively entertainment, I can promise.'

'No, no, I shouldn't wish to intrude,' said Hugh. 'It's not so far to Brendon now.'

'Well, go then, if you must; but 'tis pretty hard going, I tell yew, young man. If you should change your mind, come back and take that turning there, where you see that gurt granite post – ' he pointed to a tall stone, about seven feet high, marking a gap in the hedge where a rough track led off the lane – 'that's where 'tis, the celybration, yew know; Porton farmhouse be easy 'nough to find. Git up there, Daisy.' And on he went, his pony turning in at the granite post and disappearing from view.

Hugh marched on, but as the man had warned him, the snow was getting thicker every minute; it was wet snow too, for the weather in previous weeks had been relatively mild for the time of year and the ground was holding considerable warmth. Hugh's feet and trouser legs were soon soaked, and he began to feel faint with hunger and effort of pushing through the two- and three-feet high drifts gathering in the lane. Perhaps after all his interlocutor had been right. Where was the point in struggling on to Brendon, at least a mile and a half away?

He turned and retraced his steps, found the tall granite post and made his way down the track across two fields, though this was now covered with snow and was only discernible by some broken pieces of fencing at intervals. But soon he saw the farmhouse lights, and as he neared them he heard the sound of fiddles and people laughing and hooting as they danced.

For a few seconds he looked in through the window, seeing them stamp about the beaten earth floor of the main hall, so evidently enjoying themselves. He knocked at the door, but as it was not opened he turned the handle and went in. The warmth and loud goodwill inside hit him like a wave, and he stood blinking about him. For a few moments nobody noticed him; then the man with the dog cart broke off from dancing with a large buxom woman. 'There yew are, then, lad,' he said. 'Yew've done the right thing, coming here. I reckon we're all here for the night with this snow setting in. Are yew all right?'

For Hugh had become dizzy; the room appeared to be turning and swaying around him. The farmer himself, a thickset man of about fifty with greying hair, came forward now. 'Who's this, then, Nick?'

'A young man I met in the lane, trying to get to Brendon. I told him to come on here out of it all.'

'Quite right too,' said Samuel Weeks, the farmer. 'Get him a mug of mulled ale, he looks pretty near done in. Betty, my dear, see who's here.' They sat him down in a high-backed wooden chair.

The farmer's young wife came across and curtseyed to Hugh who, sipping the warm spicy ale they gave him, began to recover. He could not help but stare at Betty, however, which both embarrassed her slightly and amused her. 'What's up, young man? You look as if you've seen a ghost or a will o' wisp,' she laughed.

'You remind me of someone... Someone I thought I knew,' mumbled Hugh. 'Please forgive my rudeness. It is very good of you to have me here.'

'Anybody travelling in these parts is always welcome, and especially on this day of all days,' cried Samuel. 'Now make yourself at home... there's plenty of good ham and pies and lardy cake over there, just help yourself when you've a mind to. Come on, my girl, they want us to lead 'em in the Lancers.' And away the couple whirled to the music of the fiddles, played by a hoary-haired old man and a young boy sitting on stools in the corner, with foaming pots of ale before them. Across the room the logs flamed and crackled in the wide granite fireplace, sending out their generous heat. Hugh noticed, up over the chimney breast, a framed sampler worked with the words, 'The Lord seeth all that we do.' He began to enjoy the scene, deciding that the Lord must be pleased to grant Samuel and Betty happiness. After eating as much as he wanted and drinking a large glass of port which Nicholas insisted on pouring for him, he was persuaded by a jolly farmer's daughter, with a roguish twinkle in her eyes, to join the dancing.

By about ten o'clock, however, he had had enough jollity; his day's tramping on the Moor had exhausted him. He sought out his host, who said, 'Why, o' course, you must want your bed. Rachel's made up one for you.' Rachel, the elderly housekeeper and cook, showed him up the main stairs, along the landing and down a passage, then up a twisting narrow flight to one of two attics under the roof. 'We're going to be a full house tonight, sir,' she said. 'But you'll be warm and comfortable up here. There's a good feather tie on the box bed, and I've put a hot water jar in it to warm.'

She set the candle down on the chest of drawers and departed. Slowly, almost in a dream, Hugh took off his clothes, noting that they were now dry except for his stockings, the feet of which were still damp, though warm from the exercise of dancing. Across the small chamber, against the wall he saw a large carved chest of dark oak, about five feet or so long and three feet in height; above it the thatch rose across bare rafters, and the wind could be heard moaning outside. Keeping his shirt and vest on, he got into the bed, blew out the candle and sank down into the soft feather mattress, still hearing, as he lost consciousness, the vigorous rhythms of the fiddlers down below. The last thing he thought, as he drifted towards a deep heavy slumber, was that the young bride Betty, with her long dark hair and piercing black eyes, was remarkably like Lorna Doone herself as described in Blackmore's book.

He dreamed that he was lost on the Moor, wandering across hill and valley, bog and stream, with snow whirling about him in increasing flurries; the lights of a village rose before him, and he reached it, knocked on the door, and found therein Carver Doone, who seized him, bound him up and left him to starve; but the lovely Lorna herself came and gave him port wine and slices of ham and a leg of chicken. Her coal-black gleaming eyes smiled at him as she leaned forward and planted a cool kiss on his brow... Outside a loud insistent knocking was heard. Lorna vanished, fearing whoever was there. Hugh awoke.

41

There certainly was a knocking, a regular *thump, thump, thump* every second or two; and it was in the very attic where he slept. Reaching for the matches on the chest of drawers he struck one and lit the candle. There was no doubt about it; the knocking was coming from the chest across the room. Downstairs the fiddling had ceased, but he heard a great burst of laughter, as if someone had been telling a favourite joke and just delivered the punch-line.

Thump-thump-thump!

Trembling, Hugh got out of bed, went across and tried the heavy oak lid. It grated rustily as he prised it up. Inside, covered with a fine white powder, was the corpse of a middle-aged woman, laid out in a nightdress and bedcap; a grim frown of displeasure was on her pallid face. Hugh became aware of a strange unpleasant odour now permeating the room. With a cry he dropped the lid, seized his clothes and ran out of the room.

He reached the landing below, having just struggled into his trousers, when he heard the voices and footsteps of people coming up the main stairs. 'What's up, young man?' cried farmer Samuel. 'Can't 'ee sleep?'

Hugh, by now in a state of anger and shock that such a thing could happen to him, said, 'I should be glad if you'd let me sleep somewhere else. I don't take kindly to being put in the same room as a corpse.'

The convivial company – five or six of them, neighbouring farmers and their wives – stood there as if struck by lightning.

'What did you say?' Betty was the first to react.

'There's a corpse in a chest in the attic I've been sleeping in. And there were noises – knockings – I can't go back there to sleep.'

'Oh my good Lord,' groaned Samuel. 'Rachel! Where be ye, Rachel?' he shouted down the passageway.

A door opened some way along and Rachel's head, in her nightcap with untied strings hanging down, looked out. 'What is it then, Mr Weeks?'

'D'you know what you've done? You put Mr... Whatsisname here... to bed in the wrong attic. 'Twas the other one I

42

meant. You're a durned old simpleton, even if you be a good cook.'

'What's this about a corpse?' demanded Betty. 'Whose corpse? Who is it and what's it doing up there?'

Farmer Weekes sighed and looked around apologetically at them all. 'I'm sorry, good folks. I must tell 'ee how 'twas. You all here do know, except Mr...'

'Varney,' said Hugh.

'Except Mr Varney, that last winter my first wife Selina died after a long illness. 'Twas February when she went, poor soul, and we was snow-bound, far worse than this, at the time. The road was like skating rinks and the drifts was high as the hedges and higher. So us couldn't get the poor body to the undertaker and the undertaker couldn't get out to we. And then, so soon as I could venture out, there was all me sheep, dozens of 'em, lambing out in the the cold, and I was three weeks, more, seeing to 'em; and lost a pretty number for all that. So I decided the only thing to do was put poor Selina up in the attic in the old linen chest we've had for generations, and cover her up wi' salt to preserve her, d'you see, until I could get her a proper burial. Well, then I took ill wi' bronchitis for near on a month, and what wi' one thing and another, and then courting my lovely Betty here, I somehow forgot all about her... so it do seem.'

'You mean to say, she's still up there, your Selina?' Betty's voice conveyed outrage and horror. 'I'll tell you this, Samuel Weeks, whether we be married or no, I shan't stay another night under your roof, unless you promise me that soon as the weather's clear again you'll get her decently buried.'

'Yes, yes, my dear. Of course, 'twill be done so soon as I can manage now. I'm very sorry, Mr Varney, truly sorry. If only you'd listened to what I said, the other attic!' – Samuel turned on Rachel, who promptly said, 'Well, I wasn't to know what was in the box, Mr Weekes. The other attic is so draughty, too. Come along, Mr Varney, you'd better go down by the fire for the rest o' the night.'

Hugh went down to the hall, where he found a chair; and, with a rug supplied by Rachel, shared the great glowing fire, now dying slowly into a mass of rustling embers, with the

43

two sleeping fiddlers, an old sheepdog and three cats.

In the morning the snow began to melt fast with a change of wind to the west. He was glad to leave, after a silent breakfast supplied by the dourly apologetic Rachel. He left in the dog cart with cousin Nicholas, who drove him to Blackmore Gate by the lane beside the East Lyn river, now swirling fast with melting snow.

'I hope that in time you'll forgive Samuel,' said Nicholas, as Hugh got down after thanking him for the ride. 'We all have to look after ourselves as best we can in winter up here; 'tis a hard country and some queer things do happen.'

'I'll forgive him, I suppose,' said Hugh. 'But he'd better get Selina safely buried before she disturbs the house any further.'

He walked on down the road towards Barnstaple, thinking of the night's occurrences, the dancing, the woman upstairs in the chest; and of Betty with her dark flashing eyes – the eyes of Lorna Doone.

THE SEARCH FOR PERFECTION

Some critics of art these days have no use for exact representations of living objects, but I'm an artist of the old school who believes that people still want pictures that actually look like something they've seen and admired; they're mostly happier with something that seems familiar, yet is seen with new eyes. And that's the way I like to paint, rendering, according to the laws of light and colour and perspective, natural objects and persons; though, I pride myself, I do transfigure them from their ordinariness by the singularity of my vision.

Which makes my experience at Milton Abbas Lodge a remarkable one in my memory. It has a special significance for me as an artist, which will become clearer, I hope, in the telling of it.

I had been mainly doing portraits over a period of two or three years, and was making something of a name with them. I had had two successful one-man exhibitions, had sold about thirty paintings, and received commissions for nine or ten others. One of my pictures had been accepted by the Royal Academy, and one now hung in the Tate. I specialised in young people: children, boys of between twelve and eighteen, and girls and young women of considerable beauty (though always with something of real character in them). But I had certainly been overworking, and at the end of the winter was glad to accept an invitation from a friend of my days at the Slade to go down to stay with him and his wife at Milton Abbas, perched above the Devon bank of the River Tamar.

Keith and Joan Merrifield were happily ensconced in the lodge of what had once been an extensive estate; they ran an antiques business in the village, which enabled Keith to sell some of his paintings and Joan her pottery, along with the delightful collection of bric à brac, old furniture and prints in which they specialised. After more than ten years of teaching in London they had thrown everything up and decided that the country life was the answer for them. Keith couldn't praise it enough.

'It's quiet here, but not isolated – we can reach Tavistock in fifteen minutes, Plymouth in half an hour. And there's all Dartmoor up there behind us, and Bodmin Moor across the river. I'm delighted.' He was a landscape painter, and I saw evidence of his new-found love in his recent pictures of brooding tors, windswept rock-piles, and bent and twisted thorns atop stone hedges.

On my first day there Keith and I went for a fairly long hike across the moors towards Princetown; I hadn't brought an anorak with me, and had to borrow an old one of his. Unfortunately it let in a considerable amount of rain, as I discovered when, returning to the car, we encountered a series of heavy showers drifting balefully on a freshening south-west wind.

'Better have a whisky or two, and a hot bath, old chap,' advised Keith. But when we got back to Milton we found Joan was in the bathroom washing her hair (women always decide to wash their hair at the most inconvenient times, I find); and so, whisky in hand, we sat down before the empty hearth. It was striking cold at the end of that April day, and I began to shiver a little. 'I'll light a fire,' said Keith, and busied himself getting in sticks and logs; but it was half-an-hour before there was any real heat to be felt from the fireplace. When Joan appeared she said, 'I'm so sorry, Dick – if only I'd known. There isn't much hot water left, I'm afraid. Would you like a shower before dinner?'

But I was beginning to warm up now, and, the whisky loosening my tongue, I became happily involved in a lively discussion with Keith over some of the latest developments (if that is what one should call them) in art. To my mind the followers of Rothko, Hockney and Henry Moore are going nowhere – but no doubt that is exactly what they would say of my own pictures. Keith, however, does tend to go abstract once in a while, and make pretty patterns out of his fields and downs. We were still arguing, Joan joining in between dishing out paella and her special blackcurrant crumble, as we ate the meal. I retired, happily tired out, after a late bath,

46

and slept heavily for about three hours.

Looking back I see now that the chill was already then developing. My dreams were feverish, inexplicable, jumbled fragments made up of unrelated experiences merging one into another with great rapidity, some of them none too pleasant. But amid it all I became conscious of a tapping on the window. As I slowly emerged from my dream-state I thought it must be a branch scratching against the pane; I had noticed there was a japonica on the outside wall with several shoots that obscured the casement. But then I became aware that the tapping was quite regular: three beats, repeated at intervals of a second or two. I sat up; a full moon was sailing behind the trees above the cottage, as I saw through the half-parted curtains. I got out and went over to the window, with some trepidation, I admit, and cautiously looked out.

At first I saw nothing unusual. The tapping ceased; the branches of the japonica wavered a little in the slight gusts of wind, but were nodding several inches off the window pane. Softly I opened the small mullioned casement and leaned out. From below I heard what sounded like whispering; then, among the trees beyond the low wall of Keith's small garden I saw a white figure in the gloom, gesturing.

As the moon plunged behind the clouds to emerge and then disappear again I tried to focus on the figure. I am a little short-sighted, but eventually I made out the form of a girl or young woman; and she appeared to be quite naked. This is another stupid dream, I thought, my hands gripping the sill of the window, which was still wet from the rain. I closed my eyes and opened them again. She was still there, quite clearly beckoning me. She took a step forward, remaining in the shadows of the trees, and gestured again, more urgently this time. I saw she was clad in some light diaphanous material, perhaps gauze.

Now I admit that I am susceptible to the charms of the other sex, and have often been drawn into some delightful affairs with them. Most ended in pain and sorrow, though I have managed to retain some of my past lovers purely as good friends. I am not married, nor do I think I should, for some years yet, make a good husband; some other endearing creature would always distract me. But at the time of my stay at Milton I was still smarting over a brief romance which had gone disastrously wrong, and was not particularly enamoured of the idea of becoming involved with anyone else. No doubt also the gathering chill I had contracted induced a lassitude; I found myself shivering, and the thought of going down there to be embraced, or led a dance through the woods, by some unknown exhibitionist, held little appeal. 'Damn the girl, who does she think she is?' I muttered, and slowly and definitely shook my head. As I closed the window and pulled the curtains across I saw her hand drop in disappointment; she stood there for a moment and then, I saw, still looking through the inch gap left between the drapes, turned back into the wood.

I went back to bed, pulled the blankets around me and immediately lost consciousness. I slept late, and woke with a sore throat and the beginnings of a severe head cold; so, accepting Joan's solicitous suggestion, I spent most of the day in bed, dozing, reading and listening to the radio. At about five in the afternoon I got up and dressed, ate the evening meal with my hosts, and attempted further discussion; which that evening revolved around the question of whether there is any point in an artist being able to render a completely faithful representation of any object, scene or person. All art, we had to agree, is in a sense impressionism, even the most photographically accurate; and even photographs, when one came down to it, were merely mechanised impressions, though each one of a given subject changed according to light, distance, position, etc., which subtly affected the character of the subject. But I couldn't follow the threads of the argument I was trying to pursue; my mind kept wandering off at various tangents, and from time to time the image of that girl, her slender body as white as alabaster, beckoning among the shadowy trees, floated across my thoughts. I remember thinking, if she stepped out into the moonlight she would probably be a different person; perhaps a fuller light would reveal defects, or perhaps it would glorify her. Keith was saying, 'It's really the pursuit of the impossible, of course, to go on trying to define and become graphically more and more accurate; because in the end you simply can't achieve exactitude and perfection. So why not use the imagination, the freedom to interpret, even distort, in order to present one's vision?'

I had no answer just then. 'Forgive me if I go up to bed, will you? I must get the better of this cold.'

Joan produced a hot whisky-and-lemon toddy, which I was persuaded to drink, and I retired, again to drop peacefully and gratefully into the depths of warm stupor.

But at about two in the morning I became aware of that same tapping on the window. Three times it came, each set of sounds appearing, in my emerging consciousness, to be louder than the one before. Grumbling softly at being awoken, yet mightily interested, I got up and parted the curtains.

The moonlight was more brilliant than on the previous night, being unbroken; there was a cloudless sky and absolute stillness outside, which promised a frost before morning. Below in the shadow of the beeches was the girl again; but this time another one was with her: slightly more ample, though still to most minds perfectly proportioned. (These matters change continually, of course: you can't compare Twiggy or most salon models with the Naked Maja or a Rubens nude, but all in their times have been held to be the ultimate in excellence of figure). Both girls took several steps forward and beckoned, and the slender one came so far forward as to allow the moonlight under the branches to freckle her with silver-grey; I fancied she was smiling.

I was now completely awake, and very much excited. Indeed, despite my cold, I felt my desires stirring, and began to curse the indisposition which prevented me from going to join them. After all, I thought, a moonlight adventure in a strange wood with two such fascinating creatures – what Lothario could resist such an invitation? But of course it would be foolhardy in the extreme to go down in my present state. I'd come down there for a rest, for recuperation in a sense; and such an excursion was likely to land me in hospital. 'Mustn't be a damned fool,' I said firmly but regretfully to myself.

So again I opened the casement, and shook my head. But then something prompted me to express, by gestures of the hands, my regret; and I found myself blowing a kiss to each of the glimmering forms in the shade down there, and mouthing the words, 'Tomorrow night – tomorrow I'll come down.' After which, almost horrified, yet vastly intrigued at what I'd done, I firmly shut the window. This time however I closed the curtains rather more slowly; I left them about ten inches apart, and saw the girls link hands sadly and turn back among the trees. But then I noticed them look to their right, and glimpsed a dark movement of another form near them. It could have been a man, making threatening gestures, but I could not in the least be sure. Then the trees were still and uninhabited again, and not an owl nor a mouse stirred down there.

Too excited now to sleep, I lay in bed for an hour or more turning over in my mind the whole scene and wondering what it meant. Something peculiar, perhaps evil, perhaps quite harmless, was going on. Who were the girls? If that was their master I had seen, was he punishing them for coming to attract my attention? Was he dominating them in some circumstances of enslavement from which they were trying to escape? My chivalrous instincts, the product of the minor public school my parents had sent me to, were aroused. Yes, tomorrow night, come what might, I must investigate. Should I tell Keith and Joan? Doubtless they would only laugh and dismiss it all as a feverish dream. No, I would say nothing to them. Besides, the idea of a lone adventure strongly appealed to me: it would be my own personal exploration, whether I was to suffer or be rewarded by it.

I awoke late, dressed and went downstairs. Joan was busy washing clothes; I ate the solitary breakfast laid out for me. She came in as I was finishing. 'How do you feel now, Dick?'

'Quite a lot better,' I said. 'I'd like some fresh air.'

'When I've got through this lot I'll go down to the shop, and you and Keith can go out somewhere.'

When Keith arrived I was in the garden, looking over the

50

hedge and into the woods. They seemed innocuous enough from where I stood: mostly well-spaced, smooth-trunked beeches, some with moss climbing up them, the old parkland trees with some more recent growth of ash and sycamore among them. By no means impenetrable, but dense enough to be alluring and slightly mysterious. The sense of mystery could well have derived from what I'd seen the two previous nights, for the vivid shoots and fresh sun-dappled spaces, hardly glades, seemed inviting enough. Thrushes, wrens and chaffinches also found it attractive, singing and searching for insects among it all; I was contentedly staring at all this when Keith said from behind me, 'Nice bit of woodland, that. Pity they don't do something with it.'

'What should they do with it?'

'Oh, manage it properly – cut down some of the older trees and plant new ones. There's money in wood, you know. I know of craftsmen who could use a supply of good beech.'

'Who owns it?'

He shrugged. 'I've never really found out. I understand there's a sort of family trust that took over after the last resident owner died here. A queer affair, that; but another story. Now, I propose, with your approval, that we have a stroll down to Milton and a pint before lunch; then this afternoon all three of us drive up to Belstone and walk over the moor. Needn't go far from the car if you don't want to. But it'll give Joan a break.'

I meant to ask further questions about the estate and its former owner, but various other considerations – the three of us when together never had any lack of topics to discuss – seemed to obscure it. So we went off and walked five or six miles over one of the most spectacular parts of Dartmoor, returning late for an evening meal. The air cleared my nose and I felt I was now getting the better of the cold. Nevertheless I refused to be drawn into more discussions about art, and after watching an hour of fairly intelligent television (concerning the work of some creative photographers of the 1920s, which made me realise what disproportions can be achieved with the camera) I took two aspirins with a mug of hot cocoa and retired. But not to sleep.

I lay in bed and read a book for an hour, awaiting the tapping on the window. It seemed an inordinate time coming; I did not think I could sleep with the anticipation, but in fact I had dozed off, book in hand (it was the *Memoirs of Augustus John*, one of my great stars as a painter, an unconventional and highly interesting man) when, about half-past twelve, I heard it. I switched out the light and went to the window. There below, almost in the shadows, holding out their arms in clear moonlight, were *three* girls. I gasped. The moment had come.

But what if Keith or Joan were awake? I opened the casement, blew them all a kiss, and signalled that I was coming down; then looked to see if there was in fact a way down to the ground from the window. The stairs of the lodge were apt to creak, and I didn't feel I could negotiate them without advertising my movements. The japonica had a pretty stout trunk, I judged, strong enough at least to bear my weight whilst I climbed down to the kitchen roof below. I am not heavy, and keep myself in good trim by playing tennis and squash. So, pausing only to pull on a sweater over my pyjamas, I leaned out of the window and successfully swung myself down. In my excitement I gave no thought to wearing anything on my feet, but the cool wash of dew on my soles seemed to refresh and spur me on. I climbed over the low garden wall and went to meet them.

As I advanced they retired a little within the wood, but stayed there, waiting. Three of them, I thought – were there others besides? I was driven on by an insatiable curiosity, reinforced by half-suppressed sexual yearnings. Hope I'm not going to make an idiot of myself, but it's the old story, I suppose, nothing ventured...

I stepped within the silver-speckled gloom of the trees, and stood still. They came towards me, those goddesses, their pure white forms shimmering. They smiled, their eyes, hardly discernible in the gloom, full of dark dreaminess. I felt their cool hands upon me, as two of them took me by the arms and laid their cheeks against mine, one on each side of me: while the other, standing before me, put their hands on my waist and leaned forward to brush my lips gently with hers. It was a chill, fragrant touch, hardly a kiss, but full of intrigue and subtle promise. A low perfume seemed to permeate the air; I could not put a name to it, and can hardly describe it now: a muted distillation of dead rose petals and crushed primroses perhaps. It only added to the spell which, I recognised without any attempt to resist, was taking hold of me.

'We're so glad you've come,' breathed the one who had all but kissed me; she was the girl who appeared alone on the first night, the most slender and tallest of the three. Her face was perfectly oval with high cheekbones, her long honey-coloured hair hung straight down on the shoulders, and her wide eyes, grey or blue, I judged, searched into mine as if to explore my innermost depths. What utter loveliness, I thought; I hardly wished to move, and merely gazed upon her. But she turned and beckoned. 'Come, we can't stay here. You must meet the Master.'

So there was a man behind it all. Visions of a great wizard or warlock figure, dealing in magical rites, enslaving and possessing these and dozens of other gorgeous creatures, passed through my mind. But we were moving forward among the great shimmering boles of the beeches, the other two girls still gently but firmly holding me by the arms, and I did not resist.

My eyes were fixed on the form leading the way; I was fascinated, suddenly in love with the way she moved: regally, fastidiously, and then turning with a smile that seemed to promise me something personally. Her long slender back had a perfect curve that would have delighted any connoisseur of feminine beauty, her hips swayed just enough to be exciting without being too overtly sexual; her perfectly rounded hams and finely sculpted thighs moved on, with that long hair swinging gently above them, and I could have cried with delight. I glanced at the others: they kept their eyes ahead, both with a dreamy, trancelike stare, not smiling now. There was something strange about them, but in my obsession with the wonderful girl before me I could not speculate then on what it was.

We seemed to walk a long time through those woods, though I was content to follow and adore. But finally through the trees I became aware of the shadowy shape of a mansion, with lights in several rooms of one wing.

I suppose I had assumed, on the previous nights, that there was a manor house there somewhere behind the trees, but either uninhabited now or lived in by caretakers only. I had not even asked Keith about it. Living at the lodge, he and Joan paid rent to the family trust, and that was all I knew. Yet it was with no surprise at all that I accepted now that the lord of the manor, some great man, actually lived here, with his friends, attendants, or concubines. Such was the euphoric dream-state in which I was held. As we approached the house I heard music, soft and haunting, compounded of harps and woodwinds: an ancient air of great nostalgia and ecstasy, like the crying of seals off some Hebridean isle, or the ensorcelling moans of sirens in a Scillonian cave. As we came to the open main door of the house it became louder, and I was even more charmed (in the true and deepest sense of the word), fixed in the ecstatic spell they had managed to cast upon me. What on earth, I wondered briefly, is happening to me? And, does it matter? It will no doubt be a great experience. It already is.

The Master was in the hall, surrounded by dark pictures in ornate frames and tall vases with pampas grass in them, awaiting us. 'So glad you have come,' his voice boomed, with a hollow, slightly echoing sound – was it the effect of the long marble-floored hall, or a quality peculiar to itself? – 'I have long wished to meet and talk with a fellow artist.'

He was tall and stooping, with saturnine black hair and eyebrows, a long hooked nose and pointed beard; and a face ravaged by depredations I could only guess at. It was evident that he had been extremely handsome in his time; indeed the furrows and wrinkles, the lazily drooping curve of the mouth, the purple pouches under the eyes, all seemed in some perverse manner to emphasise his past magnificence rather than detract from it. He was still bodily impressive, a forceful compelling presence, and his eyes, with their light grey-green gaze, seemed to hold one in a beam of intense searching, as if he could see into one's innermost soul. The most striking thing about him, perhaps, was the long dark mane of hair, hanging down over his shoulders and beautifully cared for: a silken mass of tresses that seemed to glow with an inner suffusance, giving out tints of steel-grey, ochre and amethyst in the subdued light of the hall.

'Thank you, Merina, my dear,' he said to the leading girl, and indicated with a nod to the others they could release me. The girls left us and went inside, but not before Merina had shyly glanced back and smiled at me again.

'Come this way,' the Master now invited me, and I followed him into a salon where two more girls were waiting. They had the same pleasant, rather vacuous expression on their faces, and were in delightful gauzelike *deshabillé* like the others. 'You must disrobe, my dear sir, to take part in our hospitality.'

I realised that under the sombre cloak he wore, black and mauve with oriental emerald-green motifs embroidered on it, the Master himself was naked. I noticed hanging round his neck on a gold chain a small amulet of copper or bronze, and on it engraved a reversed swastika in a circle, with various markings around the edge.

The girls took off my pullover and pyjamas, with gentle dreamy actions, faraway half-smiles on their faces. 'Are they not delicious creatures?' the Master murmured, as if he too took great pleasure in watching them perform these actions. One of them now took a sponge, the other a towel, and from a large basin of scented water they washed me from head to foot with infinite soft caresses, as I stood there. It was indescribably enchanting, sub-erotic, blissful. Finally dried, I was touched at various intimate parts of my body with some ointment which caused me to glow radiantly within. Finally the Master, going to a closet, revealed a row of cloaks of wide-ranging hues and patterns hanging within; chose one, and put it on me himself, smiling with a deep appraisal of me as he did, as if he intended to initiate me into a sybaritic life as the acolyte of his mysteries. As he did I saw that the markings around the edges of the amulet on his chest were Ogam characters; but having then no knowledge of that ancient Irish script, I had no idea what they signified.

Both now arrayed in cloaks, mine a scarlet affair trimmed with fur and lined with blue-green shot silk, we entered a large drawing room whence the music seemed to issue. I did not discover how the distant sound, with its mysterious echoes from other worlds and the remote past, was made. I assumed it came from some recording system, perhaps a tape, though I could see no speakers; it seemed to go on and on, varying little in its mood, without interruption. I made some remark to the Master about it. 'I am glad you like my music. I have been all over the world collecting it,' he said. 'But sit and relax, and let us discuss art, which is after all the only real purpose of life.'

I was not sure that art can thus be described, though, dwelling for a moment on the thought, I had to agree that as it was what I personally was best fitted for, it was indeed my true purpose. Presumably, then, it was the Master's also. Not being disposed to argue this point, I reclined on a couch opposite one on which the Master now lay, and with six or seven lovely semi-nude girls filling our glasses with wine – and what a wine! but I shall come to that later – and plying us with choice nuts, grapes and sweetmeats, we began a long discussion of the history and movements of art that lasted, I imagined, for at least an hour.

It was, however, I soon found, a somewhat one-sided discussion; for, after my attempting to contribute a few intelligent comments, it seemed obvious that the Master's intention was to do all the talking himself. Each time I spoke he hardly allowed me to complete a sentence before indicating, with a gracious wave of his hand (hardly impatient, but clearly implying acceptance or dismissal of my remark) that he was bent on continuing. So I relaxed and listened, more and more desultorily, as his survey went on and he stared up at the sculptured ceiling, his theatrical voice rolling around the room in deep modulated tones. Soon my attention wandered. I examined the décor of the room, which was sumptuous enough; it had an oddly *fin-de-siècle* atmosphere, with its great potted palms, rubber plants and heavily striped gold and crimson wall-paper; and, yes, what was surely an Aubrey Beardsley, a reproduction of Salomé with the head of John the Baptist, hanging over the fireplace in which a massive log fire blazed.

And the girls. In turn I watched each of them, drinking in every feature of their faces and bodies, as they moved slowly, almost idly about their tasks, attending upon us or on the fire, or simply listening to the Master. There was, however, little reaction from them; no doubt they had heard his discourse often enough before; their vague half-smiles did not betray that they actually understood anything of what he was saying as he progressed with his own peculiar interpretations through the art of ancient Egypt, Greece and Rome, the medieval Churches, east and west, the Aztecs and Incas, the Chinese dynasties and the Japanese; through Renaissance, Neo-Classical and Romantic art to the Pre-Raphaelites and Art Noveau of the late 19th century, the Impressionists and Post-Impressionists, to Cubism and German Expressionism.

In a way it was magnificent. His flow of words was unabated except for the occasional sip of wine (he ate nothing, as far as I could see). But none of it quite made sense to me; his arguments, I realised when I followed them closely for a minute or so, were full of non-sequiturs and specious assumptions; it was clear to me that his preconceived ideas or obsessions were being forced into his encyclopaedic and otherwise scholarly review. One girl only seemed to react to it all – Merina, the one who had received and led me in. She nodded in agreement now and then, as if she were hanging on to every word he said; and between whiles looked at me with some hidden intent or meaning in her glance, a sort of hopeful plea in her eyes.

After a while I began to understand. She too realised, and was humouring him. Also, I began strongly to suspect, she was reacting against his domination, against the pointless services she performed here, and wished to escape. She was mutely asking for my help to get away from this situation.

The others were hardly more than mindless slaves, robbed of their personalities and wills by this egomaniac. And I noticed a drowsy feeling now creeping over me; my own will to think, to disagree with the Master's sentiments, was beginning to be sapped.

Was it the wine? I noticed that all the girls except Merina drank it from time to time. She sipped, but so little she could hardly have swallowed more than a thimbleful all evening. It was a delicious nectar, smooth and not too sweet, glowing on the tongue and in the throat as it descended to the stomach. But as one drank more that effect faded, and a stupor set in. It was like eating lotus-fruit, or taking mescalin, perhaps the Sacred Mushroom. I suddenly saw the whole establishment as a den of addicts dreaming their lives away; except for one solitary brave girl who had somehow retained her consciousness and ability to question the judge.

I wondered indeed that Merina was allowed so much independence of mind, but the truth was, as I soon realised, that whilst the others were completely docile and utterly dominated, to the point of accepting everything required of them unquestioningly, the Master required one intelligent girl to whom he could deputise the running of the house and the direction of the others in his absence, or his withdrawal to his studio. And perhaps he also needed one who could actually understand and appear to sympathise with his obsessive theories.

But what exactly was his work? I soon knew. He had been, he told me, a sculptor in his youth, and had studied under some of the most fashionable exponents of the day – which, I now realised, was longer ago than I had at first assumed. And I gathered that far from developing his art and moving into the modern age, he had become narrowly classical, and was now occupied almost solely with one fanatical purpose – to achieve the perfect representation of the female human figure in stone.

'Ah,' he sighed, turning over and over the amulet on his broad bare chest, lightly fuzzed with silver and grey hairs, 'how many times have I worked day and night on some choice block of marble or limestone, with what I felt to be the ultimate in womanly beauty standing there before me; only to realise before I completed my task that either she did not actually measure up to my ideals, or that I could not achieve in stone the perfection of my vision of her. Oh, I became famous as a sculptor of nudes – I made a fortune from it,' – he waved at the lush furnishings about him – 'I could have anything, anyone I wanted, and I indeed have had them over these many years. But in the end none of it satisfies me; everything palls, success turns sour in the mouth. I hope you never reach this state, my friend.'

'I'm hardly likely to, I think,' I assured him.

'It is hell, a living hell, believe me. I want only release from it now.' He paused and turned his terrifying searching eyes on me, and I thought, held there fascinated in his gaze, that I detected a deep and distant torment, until now unrevealed to anyone else. 'I seek only to achieve my perfect work, then it will be all over. There will, you see, be no reason for me to live after that.'

A silence. Merina came to him, as if by instinct, and stood beside him, laying her hand on his brow as if to comfort him. But she looked at me, as if saying mutely, 'This is my plight, my torture too. Help me. Help him.'

And he did request my help.

'I have resolved,' he said, when the girl had gone back to her place, 'to make one final attempt. I have at last found the means whereby I can make a completely faithful representation of any model. It requires only the finding of a suitable subject – and the decision is the hardest part. After all these years perhaps I have become satiated with near perfection, with all these attractions about me, and I can no longer judge with certainty. A second opinion is what I need: which is where you, my friend, will help.'

He said this with absolute certainty; no request, no appeal. And another swift glance from those eyes, penetrating, it seemed, to the innermost recesses of my mind, convinced me that I could not refuse; or rather, that I refused at my peril.

'I will help,' I said. 'What is it you want of me?'

'Your opinion as an artist, for I know you are a true one – not one of those charlatans who distort and break up the sacred human form for their own nefarious purposes. Merina, call the others, my dear.'

And in a moment or two there were some twenty girls in the room, of various heights and sizes, all in their ways immensely attractive, and many, to my mind, devastatingly beautiful: some distinctly buxom and heavily breasted, some slender, some short and petite yet exquisitely formed; some with long fair hair, some dark and curled, a red-head or two; some dusky complexioned and sultry, one or two like white northern goddesses. They all seemed to move well, with a graceful carriage either inborn or acquired. And all had that distant half-smile on them, and the half-dead gaze in their eyes. Except, of course, for Merina.

'Now take your time, my friend. Examine each one as long as you wish. And when you have judged which is the ultimate in perfection among them, a room is at your disposal and you may sleep with your choice tonight, before I commence the work.'

I wondered at this, but, now excited despite the effects of the wine, I rose from the couch and went among them, measuring with my eye, appreciating proportions, erectness, the structure of faces, the spacing of eyes, the curves of hips and thighs and calves. And after a cursory examination of them all I began to reject: some because of a tiny disfigurement, or lips a shade too thin or thick, one or two because their breasts or legs did not exactly match. Then, on a more personal level of choice, I discounted the smouldering beauties of the south, and also the ice-frigid deities of the north, preferring the soft modulations of the Anglo-Celtic type. One, with a daring, pixie-like face and Cupid-bow lips, a deliciously pointed bosom and narrow waist, I lingered before; but she was perhaps too short, only five feet or so in height, and I reluctantly passed her by as well. And in the end, as I had known perfectly well all along I would be, I was left with Merina. She was indeed my ideal, my ultimate, and I knew with a full surging heart that only she could hold any accolade I had to bestow. 'This,' I said to the Master, 'is the one.'

'I was afraid you would choose her. Ah well,' he sighed, 'so be it. Merina, my dear, go and prepare yourself for a night of love.'

At this Merina gave me the most intense and passionate look, full of desire but also of terror; and I stared back at her amazed, afraid to think what it meant. Her smile was gone, and all I could divine was that intensity of feeling – for me, I hoped and believed, but also for some nameless object of dread. Was she, could she be, still a virgin? After the Master's years of fulfilling every whim and wish in this isolated house, I doubted that. No; she feared much more than being deflowered, but there was no chance, it seemed, of discovering what it was then.

'Come, my dear fellow,' the Master now said, becoming suddenly and fulsomely genial, 'let me conduct you to my studio and gallery. I will show you the work of many years, and also my latest techniques.' I followed him out into the hall, along a dimly lit passage, and eventually into a long room lit by day from the south.

Here I beheld rows of statues and busts, some of marble, some of limestone, others in bronze, some only in clay; there were plaster casts and a great cauldron over a furnace, used, presumably, for melting the tin and copper. The nearest sculpture was a reproduction of the Venus de Milo. 'What do you think of her?' said the Master, caressing the lovely lines of the stomach. 'If only she had arms, eh? But look – over there – what do you say?' He had created a new Venus complete in every detail, with arms held one behind her, one in front. It was impressive, though no doubt any sculptor of proficiency could have done it. Yet the magic was missing; she was as vacuous as one of his mute girls. 'Very fine,' I murmured. 'And yet...'

His eyes flashed at me. 'And yet she is not, even now, perfect. You are right. I did this many years ago, and saw that it could not be enough. It was a mere exercise, a study, a copy of a copy, though extended and supposedly complete. No, sir, what I wanted was life, an extra nobility, a sense of breathing – indeed, a spirit in stone. That, my friend, is just

61

what I have been seeking all these years. The original Venus of course has it – she does not need arms to tell us she has eternal life. I studied and refined my art until I could reproduce her in every detail; but I could not give her that sense of being alive. And so with these others...' his eyes ranged over the thirty or forty figures, mostly of women, but some of young boys and one of a long-haired man, bearded, in a cloak, whom I recognised as the poet Algernon Swinburne '...all, all quite mathematically perfect; yet none of them with that vital attitude, that enigmatic *something* that triumphs over dead stone. And so for years, decades in fact, I pondered, and made studies, models, drawings, and researches. Now tonight you will have the great joy of Merina – and I have no greater gift to offer you. She has been my right hand, my thinking arm; but after this is achieved it will be no matter, for I will have no need of her. I shall need nothing more, except a quiet death.'

All this set me thinking again; the fumes of the drugged wine cleared from my head as I breathed the cool airy atmosphere of the gallery. What on earth was to happen? He was going to sculpt Merina: but how was he to inject life into his creation? Was he going to reveal the secret to me?

We came to the end of the gallery, where two nude female figures stood slightly apart from the rest of his work. 'At last,' he said, 'I made the discovery, unlocked the door of the great mystery. This statue,' laying his hand on the nearer of the two, 'has been commissioned by the Duke of Beaufort, and this one,' indicating the other, 'by a Mr Henry Ford, who makes motor cars, I am told, in America. I hope they will be pleased. They are not, perhaps, absolute perfection, but they have at least, do you not agree, the essential and everlasting breath in them?'

I had to agree that they had. Indeed it was wonderful to me how he had conveyed the feeling of life in those figures; and a contemplative, remotely sad sensation assailed me, in harmony with the gaze of those elegant delicate forms. One rested her hands on her hips, and looked slightly to her left, as if about to turn; the line of the shoulders was at an angle to the pelvis with one foot placed slightly behind the other.

The second figure looked down, broodingly, meditating on what sorrows I could only guess, her hands clasped before her, with her head bent at an exquisitely graceful angle. I went close to the figures, walking around them. I could have believed, without any great effort, they were actually breathing; indeed I put my hand on them, tracing their sensuous lines, half-expecting the stone to yield like flesh under my fingers.

'You see,' the Master laughed, a half-manic lilt in his voice, 'I have discovered the secret at last. Now there is only one more thing to do; to produce Merina, the perfect woman, in stone.'

I ran my fingers pensively down the sides of the two figures. In stone, he said; yet this material did not feel like stone. It had a warmer, more malleable quality. 'What sort of stone is this?' I asked.

'Aha. Now that, indeed, would be letting out the secret I have sought for so long. You really cannot expect me to tell you that, after these years of strivings, can you? No, no, my boy. The secret of the stone will die with me. But ah, if only Michelangelo and Phidias had known it, what even greater masterpieces would they have bequeathed the world!'

He was leading me back now. 'Come, come, do not bother yourself with mere details. The lovely Merina awaits you, for a last night of delight and fulfilment!'

'Why do you say a last night?' I asked, innocently enough, but beginning to suspect some horrible intent on his part. He paused, fixed me in his grey-green luminous stare; his eyes enlarged and a vein stood out pulsing on his forehead. Then he relaxed and smiled. 'Why, just a manner of speaking,' he said. 'When the work is completed she will be released from my service, as they all will be. I shall have no need of any of them again. Come.'

So we left the gallery and walked back along the dark passage, to the main hall where that wistful haunting music still played from its unknown source, and he gave me into the charge of two of the girls, who conducted me up the stairs. 'Goodnight, my dear friend... I shall be eternally indebted to you,' he called. I looked down, to see him smiling, his teeth gleaming amid the black beard, the amulet glinting on his chest, as the folds of his cloak hung open. Then he turned and strode into the salon wherein we had talked.

The two silent girls led me up to the first floor, along a deeply-piled carpet around a landing, and down a short corridor to a bedroom door which was slightly open. They paused, smiling sadly, uninterestedly, indicating that I was to enter. I pushed open the door and there was Merina, sitting on the bed, her hands clasped before her, awaiting me. She sprang to her feet and in a second we were locked in a passionate embrace, lips to lips, breast to breast. 'Oh my dear, my dear,' she breathed. 'We must not waste time. It is long past midnight, and at dawn he will come for me...'

I paused, looking at her, and released her a little from my clasp. 'Why are you so afraid of him... or of what is going to happen?'

'Don't ask,' she said. 'Accept the gift he has made you... the gift I shall make you, of myself... for it is all we can do. Whatever else will be, will be. At least I shall not go on living in that way, forever attending to his wants and pleasures.'

She was drawing me to the bed, and I allowed myself to be divested of the cloak; then we lay there in each other's arms, the magic of her cool fragrant quintessential womanliness overcoming me. 'Love me, love me,' she whispered. 'Oh my darling, love me truly and well.'

And I may say, without undue pride or vanity, that I did so. I think I have never loved anyone so well, nor ever shall again. She drew from me the most glorious expression and desires of manhood; I excelled myself and utterly fulfilled her, time and again. O Merina, truly were you perfection among women! Perfection of personality, sympathy and erotic bliss, as well as of bodily form.

After some two or three hours, as I guess, we lay still and slept in each other's embrace. I awoke first, and in the moonlight filtering through the curtains watched her face, laid on my breast, and saw a smile of deep satisfaction there. But then, as I looked, her eyes opened and she stared at me, with an unutterable yearning and regret for what could never be repeated. I knew there was something to be unravelled, some infamous plot in which she somehow shared, to her own detriment or destruction, but which she was sworn (being dominated, perhaps brainwashed) not to reveal. And the thought that this love of ours was never to be continued, that having found I was to lose her, was more than I could bear to contemplate.

'Tell me now,' I said. 'What is he going to do with you?'

She stared at me, half-hoping, half in horror. 'I can't tell you.'

'But you know what it is.'

'I know, well enough.'

'It's something to do with those two statues, the latest two he's so proud of.'

Her silence was assent enough. My brain began to work unbidden, concentrating on the problem. 'The stuff he sculpted them from... it isn't actually stone, is it?'

Minutely she shook her head.

'It felt like...' I searched for a comparison. '. . . some plastic material; something easily worked and moulded... like a quick-drying cement of some kind.'

She stared at me, her eyes urging me on; perhaps some thought transference took place between us, because suddenly I saw it all. 'Those girls... the models for the two statues... they're there, aren't they? Inside the casing which has become the sculpture. My God... he's either insane or the devil incarnate! He's sculpting on to living human flesh. And I suppose they were in such a trance they couldn't react to prevent it.'

She was weeping now in mute agreement, terrified of this fate which was shortly to be her own. Her cold salt tears welled up and fell on my chest, and she shook and sobbed against me. I was in a fury now. 'It won't happen to you; not while I'm here!'

She looked up piteously. 'He'll kill you, and me as well, if we oppose him.'

'We'll escape before he comes.'

'How?'

I considered. There was no daylight yet, only the fading moon, as far as I could see. We might have an hour, perhaps half an hour, before he came for her. 'There must be a way out of this place.'

'He knows everything that goes on in the house.'

I got up and went to the window. There was a fifty feet drop to the gravel of the terrace below. We had to get down, reach the woods, and escape... 'There must be a back door, or kitchen entrance,' I said.

'There's a small staircase at the end of this corridor; it leads down to the stables. The door is bound to be locked, though.'

'Come on,' I said, full of decision now. 'Let's go down and try it.'

We put on our single garments, I the sleek cloak the Master had given me and she a gown we found in the wardrobe in the room, and we crept noiselessly out, along the corridor, and down the narrow stairs to the stone-flagged ground floor.

We found the back door, but it was firmly locked and there was no key. It was a thick oak construction of no great antiquity, and clearly would have been impossible to break down without an axe. But the little room next to the passage had a small sash window, which, when I tried it, yielded not an inch, its catch being rusted solid, and the timber frames swollen. There was no help for it: the glass must be broken. Aware that someone, the Master himself no doubt, would hear, I knew I had to act swiftly. I took up the doormat lying by the oak door and, placing it against the window, beat on it with my fists, breaking the glass which tinkled out on to the mossy cobbled court outside. Then laying my cloak, folded, across the lower edge of the window so that we should not suffer lacerations, I helped Merina through the small aperture, then followed myself. Once out in the court we fled, hand in hand, across the terrace, down through the rose garden, and beyond into the park. Soon the great beeches were about us, and as we ran I noticed the first glimmerings of dawn through their branches.

I confess I really did think we had managed it. We ran and

ran until, almost exhausted, I stopped, panting painfully, and leaning against a tree, clasped my love in my arms. And then, as we stood there recovering our breaths, we heard someone running towards us through the verbiage.

It was the Master. Naked except for the amulet, his black hair streaming out, insensate fury in his eyes, he burst into the glade where we stood. He was unarmed and, dazed as I was from running, for the moment I saw no need to flee. I was wrong, though looking back there was little we could do about it. With an unsuppressed animal roar he leaped upon Merina, his hands closing around her beautiful delicate neck, in an unrelenting grip of strangulation. I closed with him and tried to prise his hands open: his grasp was superhumanly fierce, and my puny efforts made no impression on him whatever. His eyes rolled and seemed about to come out of his head in a terrible epileptic rage: indeed he was foaming at the mouth, his teeth bared like those of some saturnine creature from the underworld. I let him go and picked up a heavy branch that lay nearby. Once, twice, thrice I raised it and brought it down on his skull; and still he stood there, the girl by now suffocated in his grip, her neck broken, but unable it seemed to let her go. Then, as I levelled the branch to charge him in the small of back, he suddenly threw her aside onto the ground, her head lolling limply upon her shoulders, and turned the maniacal fury of his glare upon me.

I admit I was horrified, indeed, possessed by a nameless dread I hope never to experience again. His eyes, flecked with blood, bulged out above the slobbering mouth and long pointed yellow teeth; I understood the awful terror and domination he had exerted on his minions, and knew that if I let myself look into his gaze a moment longer I should be lost. Dropping the branch I turned and ran. How long I ran, so fleet of foot it seemed to me I was flying over the ground and hardly touching it, my bowels melting with fear within me, I do not know. Perhaps not more than a minute or so. Whether he pursued me I cannot recall. But negotiating the great exposed roots of a fallen sycamore which had succumbed to some past storm, I tripped, fell, hit my head on an outcrop of granite, and immediately lost consciousness.

☆☆☆

I emerged again to sentient life to find I was in the bed I had occupied at the lodge. Late afternoon sunlight was beaming redly through the woods beyond the little mullioned window and, apart from a few chirrupings of birdsong and a lorry passing along the road, all was silence. I moved and felt a searing pain shooting through my head; and became aware of a tightly wound bandage around my forehead. Gradually I put together in my mind the events, presumably of the previous night, which had led up to the accident. I felt sheer desolation at the thought of that marvellous girl, Merina, who must surely have been killed by that monster. To whatever stroke of fortune or intervention by the gods I owed my own escape, I could not guess; but I knew that the Master's intolerable egocentricities must be brought to an end: he must be brought to law and locked away for life.

At that point, my head throbbing with the effort of thinking, I could only contemplate telling Keith and Joan of my adventure, and informing the police. I must have passed out again, because it was dark when I next remember my friends beside me, Joan holding my hand and saying, 'You'll be all right, Dick dear. The doctor will be here again in the morning.' She made me sit up and sip tea, which I managed without too much pain and difficulty. Propped up against the pillows I felt clearer in the head, and said, 'Where did you find me?'

'Just outside the garden hedge,' Keith said. 'You've got twelve stitches in your head, and you lost quite a lot of blood. Thank God I heard your shouting, or you might have been there till morning bleeding to death.'

'Shush, Keith,' Joan said firmly. 'Let him rest.'

Indeed I had closed my eyes. But all I could see was Merina's imploring face, her confidential smile, and the images of our lovemaking the night before.

A little later they gave me some food, and a powerful sedative which sent me into a death-like sleep for about twelve hours. I was awakened at ten the next morning by the doctor from the village, who pronounced me fit enough but in need of at least a fortnight's rest, and who prescribed more drugs. But I had to get my story out, and when he had gone I said to Keith and Joan, 'Now look, I have to tell you what happened. You must listen. It's very important, and you'll see why. So don't tell me to rest until you've heard it all.'

They sat down by the end of the bed and listened, saying nothing until I finished. Then they looked at each other, Keith smiling slightly, Joan looking puzzled. Keith said, 'Well, there's no need for the police, Dick. The house burned down sixty years ago and your Master, the owner, died in the fire. But it's certainly a strange thing...'

'Incredible,' Joan said. 'They found the bodies of ten or more young women there, I heard. Some escaped though, I believe.'

'Sixty years?' I repeated. 'Then there's nothing there?'

'Only ruins. You can go and see for yourself when you're up and about again.'

Which in a week or so, I did. Meanwhile, through Keith, who asked further of the older inhabitants of Milton, I gleaned what I could of the celebrated affair of the Manor House. A yellowed cutting from the Western Morning News was lent by someone, and the whole situation became much clearer.

It transpired that the Master (whose name was Eric Deauville Mantissa) actually had been a very successful sculptor during the 1890s and early 1900s. But, with naturalism and representational art becoming obscured by cubism, surrealism and Dada, and the rise of modern sculptors with new approaches, he had gradually withdrawn into a world of his own at the Manor, surrounded by models for whom he advertised, and who, once engaged, were never seen again outside the grounds of the park. It had got to be a scandal locally, with all kinds of murmured accusations being made as to what went on inside there; no one, it seemed, actually knew, because no local person was employed there, and the Master was careful not to engage any girl from the district near Milton. Supplies of food and household items were either sent down from Harrods or Fortnum's, or delivered at the lodge and taken in by whoever lived there then. No one from the House or lodge ever attended church or chapel, which of course aroused grave suspicions. The Vicar, on calling, got no farther than the lodge gate, being informed that the Master was unable to receive anyone. Over several years rumours of orgies and corrupt practices, witchcraft and so on, had incensed the villagers; until one night in 1923 the Manor House was burned down. How the fire started was never officially decided; but people still hinted in the village that they knew who had been responsible.

When I recovered enough to move about I was eager to visit the site; so one morning, with Keith, I walked into the park, and we made our way through the tangled sprouting saplings and undergrowth, to the blackened and half-demolished walls of the house.

The whole extent of the building lay before us, most of its rooms still marked out by the masonry that was left; though the vegetation had long since invaded them, and sturdy sycamores and beeches now grew within the hall and kitchen and various chambers. I found what seemed to be the wing in which the Master had entertained me and, still marvelling at those ravages of time (which to me appeared to have all happened in a few days and nights), picked my way among them, wondering if I should discover anything which in any way supported my experience.

Coming upon what had evidently been the long gallery, I had a great *frisson* of horror and expectation, for there, half-covered by brambles, creeping toadflax and ivy, were the limbs and torsos of sculptures. Carefully I bent down, pulling back the undergrowth: Keith helped me, and together we assembled various arms, legs and bodies, and a head or two: still smoke-scorched, or covered with lichen or blotched with fungi. I had the terrible expectation that one or two of them, within the shells of concrete or cement which the Master had invented, would contain the rotting remains of human flesh and sinews. But, thank heaven, we found nothing of that. I reflected that his formula had been

70

for a somewhat soft, plastic and workable substance; recalling the feel of it as I ran my hands up and down those living statues, I realised that it must have melted in the blaze, and the poor bodies of entranced girls within it had perished in the inferno: my Merina among them, for I had no doubt that the Master had returned with her broken body and completed his great design.

But, as we turned to leave, something caught my eyes, gleaming dully from under a nettle leaf: I picked it up, to find it an almost shapeless lump of bronze, with part of a fine gold chain still attached to it. And in one corner of the almost fused mass were the engraved and cryptic strokes of Ogam writing. It was the Master's amulet, almost beyond recognition, and allowing no possibility of deciphering the ancient script upon it. But it was enough proof for me.

I still have that relic today, and whenever I take it into my hand it seems to suffuse me with the decadent sumptuous life within the Master's enclave, and I see him lying there on the couch, turning the burnished charm over and over as he gave out his obsessive insane discourse, while those lovely dreamlike figures hovered about us. Then my thoughts inevitably turn to Merina, and I see her dear pleading gaze again, and feel her arms about me; and I put the amulet away, choking back tears.

NIGHT ON ROUGHTOR

One summer day in the late 1960s, three young men from one of our most venerated universities came up the steep hill road from Trebarwith Strand. They carried towels and swimtrunks and their long hair was damp and uncombed. One smoked a heavy pipe with a bowl like a small incinerator; one had a bushy ginger moustache and sideboards. The third, a dark intellectual with steel-rimmed spectacles, wore a denim shirt and cap. June bloomed benevolently round them, fresh from their finals. Thick-fingered mesambryanthemum hung from walls and rock-faces, and on the deep valley slope were the minute balloons of birdsfoot trefoil, yellow and orange and shrivelling red. Viper's bugloss reared bold blue spires lower down.

'The next question is,' said Browne-Smythe in his lazy cultured tones, 'where do we go from here?'

'I suppose it'll have to be camping,' said de Vere Ellis, viewing the scene through his glasses. 'Not that I'm enthusiastic; the Cornish summer's likely to turn damp when you least want it to...'

'But where do we camp?' said Browne-Smythe, puffing slightly through his moustache. 'Come on, Mac; you know the place.'

'Thus speaketh the psychologist,' remarked McMahon, taking the huge pipe from his mouth. 'He must know where we're going. My dear chap, don't you ever feel like taking pot luck? Why not just load up the old jalopy and pitch tent wherever we get to at nightfall?'

'Any chance of camping here in the garden – or would your family object?' asked de Vere Ellis.

'Not a hope,' said McMahon. 'My old man's the trouble; wants it peaceful when he brings this dear old tycoon down. Sir Geoffrey Pomphrett, Bart. About ninety, as far as I can gather. Don't suppose the old boy would care, but fathers of my generation are a bit down on denims and long hair, that sort of thing.'

They turned in at the gate of the villa, spread their towels and costumes out on the privet and azalea bushes to dry, and went inside.

'What time's the family comin', Mr McMahon?' asked the woman who was sweeping out the hall and porch.

'Oh, any time after tea. About seven, perhaps,' said McMahon.

'Ah well,' she said, 'better go up an' air the beds, I s'pose.'

McMahon looked at his watch.

'Half-past twelve,' he murmured. 'What's for lunch, Mrs Tregellas?'

'Pasties,' she said as she stooped down with the pan brushing dust into it.

'Ha!' cried de Vere Ellis in his best mock-Cornish accent, 'Carnish Pasties, eh? Ess, me dear, tull do.'

'Not for half-hour yet, though,' said the housekeeper, unamused. 'They beds d'come first.'

The three wandered into the lounge and amused themselves drinking beer and playing gramophone records. They had the latest hit, in which an ecstatic pop-star yelled:

> 'Oh darling, oh sweetest,
> My life, my all completest,
> What'll I do without you –
> What'll I do without you?'

to an accompaniment of wailing electric guitars and shrieking saxophones.

When they sat down to the meal and, with knives and forks, had consumed the pasties, Browne-Smythe suddenly said to Mrs Tregellas as she cleared away the plates, 'Where would you suggest we go to camp for tonight?'

She stopped and said, 'I dunno, I'm sure. Never go camping meself.'

'No,' said Browne-Smythe. 'But what about the moors?'

'Aw, no,' said Mrs Tregellas. 'Not there, I wudden go there for the golden calf hisself. Not tonight, anyway.'

'Why's that?'

'Tis dangerous for one thing. All they marshes and holes.

And besides, 'tis Misummer's Eve.'

'Come, Mrs Tregellas,' smiled McMahon. 'You aren't superstitious, are you?'

'No,' she said, 'not more than anybody else is round here. I dun't take no account of talk about piskies an' giants an' ghosts, but I wudden walk through the churchyard at midnight, not fer nobody: an' I wudden go up on the moors, an' specially not near Roughtor on Midsummer night. Call me simple an' mazed if you like – but I wudden do it, I tell 'ee; an' if you go an' do it, you'm very silly.'

De Vere Ellis, who was a physicist and subscribed to those theories which explain everything in material terms, was interested. 'It's merely a question of fear,' he said. 'Your reason tells you that there's nothing in these stories of the supernatural; it's only your unreasonable subconscious self that makes you afraid of these things, as our professor of psychology' – indicating Browne-Smythe – 'will tell you.'

'Just one of the lingering hereditary animal instincts which are in process of disappearing, Mrs Tregellas,' Browne-Smythe assured her with faint amusement.

'Quite,' went on de Vere Ellis. 'We know a little too much about the subject to fear it. There's never been any ghost that couldn't be explained quite simply and reasonably. Personally, I rather enjoy disobeying superstitions; though I never walk under a ladder at any price. I once got a pot of paint down my neck... Is Roughtor a hill?'

'Ess,' said Mrs Tregellas. 'You can see it if you walk up on to the high ground up by Lob's Cot. But if you got any ideas about camping there tonight you better put 'em right out of yer head. 'Tis dangerous, I tell 'ee.'

'If Roughtor's only a hill, Mrs Tregellas,' said McMahon, 'it must be easy to climb. It'll be a fine night: the weather forecast is good, and there's an anticyclone just now.'

'No,' she said folding her arms, 'I dun't like it. I dun't like it wan bit.'

She stared out of the window to where between the roofs of other villas there were glimpses of leaning cliffs, and Gull Rock a quarter of a mile out in the torpid sheen of Atlantic waters.

'Tis no place for you,' she said. 'What about they Jacky Lanterns?'

'Just marsh gas,' said McMahon. 'Burning methane. We shan't be fooled by them any more than by Tregeagle himself.'

'Who's Tregeagle?' Browne-Smythe asked, fingering his red moustache delicately.

'Oh, a giant ghost the Cornish say runs wild on the moors, shrieking and yelling – or something of the kind. Is that right, Mrs Tregellas?'

'So the story do go,' she said. 'But he dun't run wild as rule – he've got jobs to do, like baling out Dozmary Pool with a limpet shell. They put un out here on the Strand once, so they say, to bind sand into sheaves. He managed it by wetting 'em with water on a winter's night so they froze. He's ony s'posed to run wild when he do disobey the devil. Then the hell hounds come after un. But 'tis ony the wind an' storm really, I s'pose.'

'Of course, of course,' said de Vere Ellis as he folded his napkin.

'Still, I dun't think 'tis right for you three young gentlemen to go up there. Is it Roughtor you'm thinking about? Cause if 'tis, well all I can say is you'm all three of you furriners when it come to the point, and where none of our crowd 'ud set their foot after sundown you certainly never ought to. Besides, Roughtor do mean something to we people, and some 'ud call it near sacrilege for you to camp there.'

McMahon got up, smiling. 'You Cornish are all the same: living in the past, born with your heads looking over your shoulders. All these legends and mysteries are all very picturesque, but they won't get you anywhere. I consider it'll be a bit of a lark to pitch camp on Roughtor on Midsummer Night. Anyway you needn't worry, Mrs Tregellas: my grandmother was Cornish, so I'm entitled to play the host and entertain friends, even on the holy of holies.'

McMahon's father was half-Cornish, half Irish. His mother was French. He called himself an Englishman.

'Huh! A fat lot you knaw about legends, Mr McMahon, being away up country all the year. As for whether they'll get us anywhere, well p'raps they wun't. P'raps we dun't want to get nowhere. Cornwall's good enough for me; 'tis good enough for half London in summer, seemin'ly. When my old grandmother was dying up to Tavistock they said to her, "Well, Mrs Pengelly, you'm going to a better land." An' she looked up 'an said, "Ess, there's no place like Cornwall." '

She smiled and then went on seriously. 'But I bain't joking about Roughtor. Sneer about the past if you like; but once you get up there you'm going to find what's past id'n so dead after all. Thass where 'tis; now go an' do what you like: I been yammering here too long. Let me get on with they dishes.'

Gathering up the pile of plates she marched out with the dignity of a duty done.

☆☆☆

It was about half-past seven when they set off for Roughtor, the old Ford Zephyr groaning up the hill with the weight of baggage and three university rugby forwards. At the wheel McMahon smoked placidly, the great pipe pushed out of the corner of his mouth so that it should not obscure his view. Browne-Smythe sat beside him and on the back seat de Vere Ellis held steady an ancient camp stove, found in the garage of the villa, which threatened to discharge paraffin if allowed to move off its balance.

'Oh darling, oh sweetest,
My life, my all completest...'

mooed Browne-Smythe.

'Bi-dah-bih-dah-bi-doop,' supported de Vere Ellis, tattooing on the stove with a spoon. 'Bi-doom-doom-blah-ah-ah!'

They had the windows open and the breeze never absent from the moors came flapping in. As they reached the level high ground – McMahon wrenching the gear lever, which produced a grinding protest from the engine – a few other cars passed them, their windscreens flashing red in the lowering sun. Down into grey narrow Camelford they went,

76

and beyond through valleys and up hills until the road ended abruptly at a gate opening on to the moors. On the other side of the shallow valley was Roughtor, with its crest broken, jagged like the backbone of a skeleton saurian.

They got out and unloaded. McMahon locked the car doors, lifted the bonnet and dismantled the petrol lead. He put it in his knapsack and shut the flange. They could not carry everything at once, so leaving Browne-Smythe stretched out on the turf guarding the gear – although there was nobody nearer than the farm a mile away – the others started off.

They reached the bottom of the valley and crossed the little bridge over the stream. Suddenly McMahon stopped.

'Hullo! What's that?'

'You mean that rumbling?'

'Yes. There's no railway line around here, is there?'

De Vere Ellis hauled out the Ordnance Survey map from the pocket of his large sheepskin jacket. 'No,' he said.

They stood still, the sound rushing and eddying round them. It appeared to come from farther up the valley, so they walked a hundred yards up towards it. There they found the stream plunging over a waterfall into a narrow deep pool, a small pot-hole. This must, they thought, be the source of the noise; there was no other explanation. Yet as they stood there twenty yards from it across the bog they could not say with conviction that it was definitely the cause; for the rumbling swirled round them enveloping the place, coming on them from all sides, hollow and uncanny.

'Hm,' grunted de Vere Ellis, and scratched his head.

'Come on,' said McMahon, almost as if he were glad to go and wanted to forget it.

They climbed stolidly up the hillside, the loud burbling receding below them. The grass of the lower slopes gave way to bracken and ankle-deep ling. It took them half an hour to reach the top.

Great boulders of grey granite crowded the peak. They looked for a sheltered place, but there seemed to be none. Cold evening wind hurtled across, singing between stones.

They climbed across to the eastern side where they found a rock shoulder with a small cave hollowed out on the leeward side; here it was calm like the still centre in a whirlpool. This was the place to pitch the tent. They had some difficulty in wedging the poles into the rocky soil, but with exertion they succeeded.

De Vere Ellis went back to help Browne-Smythe up with the remaining gear. Left alone, McMahon secured the tent. He hammered in pegs, fixed guy ropes, laid out ground-sheets inside and took in all the tins and apparatus they had brought. He tried to dig a rain trench round the tent but could not manage it. Then he took a long thick peagreen scarf from his haversack, a pair of binoculars, and wandered around the summit. It was nearly dusk and the sun was going behind another tor to the west, throwing it into bold black relief.

Below him shadows were lengthening second by second, creeping across moor and marsh and up the sides of hills like vast grey ghosts. Standing on the brow overlooking the precipitous west end, he could see vague standing stones in a circle immediately beneath. In daylight no doubt they would look mundane enough, but here in twilight their very vagueness seemed to promise life: at any moment they might begin to shuffle and dance. A half-forgotten tale about maidens changed into stones for dancing on the Sabbath came back to him.

Further westwards there was a huge white hill, a china claytip which by its incongruity attracted his attention. Perhaps it was a mile off, but he could not say because at every second it seemed to be a different distance away. It was a hill without roots or foundations; one that lurked and loomed, having no fixed place for its being. He found it disturbingly easy to imagine it approaching, stealing nearer and then slipping away among the other tors, all fast losing their identities in the gloom.

He looked across to his left and regarded Brown Willy, the other twin Cornish mountain. It was supposed to be higher than Roughtor, but it seemed not as tall; it sprawled loosely and carelessly against the blue night, less forceful than

78

Roughtor and more welcoming. McMahon found himself wishing they had chosen it for a camping site instead.

Roughtor and its surroundings, he saw, was a place to reckon with. All around him were stones erected in illogical positions by pristine natural forces. He found the Logan Rock, a great flat cap of stone balanced on a much smaller rock: balanced with such precision that he could rock it unaided, though it had withstood aeons of wind and storm. Like all the other rocks on this precipice it was worn smooth, rutted and grooved by centuries of wind and rain. Roughtor was ageless, barbaric, primitive; yet primitive in a positive sense, because it seemed to possess the elements of a civilisation – although one alien and opposed to his own.

Now conflicting thoughts came to him, unreasonably and without his summoning them. It was as though he stood the rock of eternity, and mere time was below him; in this sudden elevation of his historical perspective, the millenia ago that ancient men raised those stones and dolmens and barrows seemed no farther away than last week. He had an ill-defined sense of having been here before. He felt he knew the place, and he could almost have shouted out the very day – or was it century? – that he had been there; but the half-memory struggled in vain to free itself. Among these twilight thoughts, which welled up in his mind as his flesh chilled and goosed in the night wind, was an insistent discord saying he had no right to be there at all; there was also a very simple, perhaps childish, fear of some dark retribution for breaking a fundamental natural law. Then again, without his consciously thinking, a voice spoke within his mind, so suddenly like a shout in his ear or a tap on his shoulder that he started. It was the voice of Mrs Tregellas saying, 'What's past id'n so dead after all.'

Real voices now called out to him. Turning he saw a torch flashing and caught a glimpse of de Vere Ellis' blazing shirt and fleecy jacket. He groped his way back around to the tent and found his two friends putting down the remainder of the gear – bedrolls and blankets.

'We saw a will o' the wisp,' cried Browne-Smythe.

He spoke excitedly, so that the other two recoiled silently.

'Old Bertie here started the damned thing,' said de Vere Ellis in exaggerated laconic tones. 'Lit a match for a smoke as we started up the hill. Must have ignited a pocket of marsh gas.'

'Gave me quite a jolt, actually,' said Browne-Smythe. 'One second there was nothing there, and the next this kind of purple ghost was dancing like a monkey around us. Burnt out after a few minutes, of course.'

They busied themselves arranging the tent. McMahon lit a couple of hurricane lamps and tied them to the tent poles. No one spoke; they were perhaps a little fearful of betraying the fact that the place was affecting them strongly. Each knew that this night on Roughtor was going to be far less of a joke than they had imagined; but no one would admit it. Conversation was therefore strained, and confined to matters of immediate concern; which was mainly the cooking of supper. De Vere Ellis made a brave show of being at home by whistling the tune of 'Oh Darling, Oh Sweetest,' as he fried sausages over the stove, but soon he too relapsed into moody silence.

Supper over, they prepared to turn in. It seemed to all three that they could feel the proximity of the big rock that shielded them from the wind, even within the tent. It was as though it had a personality of its own which would not permit them to forget it. Probably this annoyed Browne-Smythe; he went outside for a smoke before sleeping.

Leaving the tent he frightened several rabbits which had gathered curiously outside, attracted by the faint lamplight. They went off scuttling down across the hillside. The moon had risen, full and ominously amber. There were no clouds, and shining the powerful torch down into the valley between the two hills he detected an answering shimmer from the stream that flowed through it. He shone the torch around to amuse himself: the beam reached well up the side of Brown Willy, and he saw a hump on the eastern end of it which appeared to be a barrow. One or two purple will o'the wisps hovered momentarily out beyond the marshes, and knowing what they were he now smiled superciliously; then he had a great fright, for randomly turning the beam on an outcrop of rock fifty yards away he was confronted by a white face and two large horns. For a second he stood thunderstruck, the light wavering in his hand; then he heard a deep cry, half-bray and half-bleat, and a goat leaped away over the boulders.

There was no sound except for the unwavering high note of the wind. For a moment something akin to fear gripped him, and as suddenly released him. A man could go mad on these moors, he decided. The moon cast enough light to present those gaunt shapes, grey enigmas, but never enough to explain them. Browne-Smythe threw away his cigarette and went to bed.

They lay for an hour or more sleepless on the hard ground, which their sleeping-bags did little to soften. They stared up at the indistinct canvas, listening to the wind, and each sensed the others were awake. Once McMahon said, trying to sound irritated, 'Don't go much on the orchestrations up here,' – but neither of the others replied.

The wind did however gradually die away; it was a process so slow that their minds, becoming less preoccupied with its sound, were lulled to sleep as it waned. The other two had relapsed into an uneasy slumber when de Vere Ellis sat up in bed and whispered, 'For God's sake, what's that?'

McMahon stirred and made a grunt of interrogation, then he too sat up and listened. There was a sound of laughing; or was it singing? It was both: a crowd of voices laughing and singing very close at hand.

There was nothing at all uncanny in the sounds; they were jolly voices that made them, and it was only the unexpectedness of hearing them that made the three stare at each other for minutes before anybody spoke again.

Browne-Smythe was fully awake. He did not sound afraid when he said, 'Here, I'm going out to have a look.' He dragged on his jeans and a pullover; the others followed suit.

When they got outside the revelry was loud and boisterous. The moon was clear and white again; they climbed across the backbone of rocks of the hill and were staggered by what they saw.

There were perhaps fifty dancers in a circle, with arms interlinked, leaping and jigging with tremendous energy around a big boulder, on which sat three figures. None of the dancers seemed to be over two feet high; they were all dressed in tight garments and little pointed caps of light green or blue. Their faces, even in the half-light, were shining and jovial. They sang as they danced, the little men on the boulder taking in turns to sing the verse and the whole crowd joining in the chorus with a roaring flourish. What was so stupendous, when the watchers overcame their initial surprise, was that the voices which came from the tiny beings were so loud and rich, an unhesitating unrestrained bass. What they sang none of them could understand. McMahon first thought the language was Welsh; but looking back realised it could only have been Cornish.

The three watched with a kind of astonished delight, for such merriment they had never imagined. It was naive spontaneous pleasure that spelled them motionless like statues there on the great stones. None of the rollickers took any notice of them.

This went on for some minutes, when, having become intoxicated with the mirth they saw before them, they were totally unprepared for what happened next.

Clouds passed overhead obscuring the moon, and for a half a minute there was darkness. The singing and dancing ceased abruptly; McMahon thought he saw figures stealing hurriedly away. Then they heard another song, as vigorous as the first but higher pitched and somehow more disturbing; it contained a subtly menacing rhythm; as it approached a sense of vicious or evil intent assailed them. Then the moon was freed and showed them about twenty little men no bigger than the others, dressed in the same way except that they had dark caps of black or deep blue. But the main difference was not of dress or form. These were ugly little creatures with spindly legs and square heads too large for their bodies. When the moonlight revealed them they were not so much dancing as fighting among themselves and tripping each other up in malevolent sport; but they soon saw the three humans watching them stupefied from the boulders, and with shouts of diabolical glee bounded toward them in a body.

Unable to control his actions, McMahon turned and fled. De Vere Ellis, afraid but still proud, hesitated. Browne-Smythe started to run with McMahon, but caught his foot in a crevice and fell. Four of the goblins were on him instantly, two twisting his foot, one pulling his ears and poking at his eyes, the other jabbing him with a sharp stick. De Vere Ellis took a stride towards them, sent one sprawling with a kick and clouted the others with his fists. Browne-Smythe got to his feet and they both ran.

They were going over the hillside towards Brown Willy, but McMahon's voice shrieked out urgently, 'Here! To the tent, *quickly*! We're safe here!'

The tent was not more than a hundred yards away, and they sprinted frantically across, reaching it as the crowd of little people came hopping and screeching over the rocks. They stopped ten yards away from the tent and stood around it in a ring, glowering and uttering cries of chagrin. It was as though there was a circle drawn round the tent into which they could not penetrate.

The three flung themselves down inside the tent, panting feverishly. 'Safe – safe, thank God!' gasped Browne-Smythe. He felt his scratched and torn ear, and pulled up his shirt revealing little red weals and cuts bleeding on his ribs.

With the aid of his torch McMahon was looking at the map. 'Thought so,' he said relievedly. 'This spot is marked "Chapel" here. It – this cave thing – is a chapel to Michael the Archangel, patron saint of Cornwall; so I've heard. It explains why they can't hurt us in here.'

As though they had heard the name of Michael spoken, the crowd outside dispersed silently and loped back over the boulders into the night. Once again there was silence except for the wind, which seemed to be rising, and the hard breathing of de Vere Ellis and Brown-Smythe.

'I once went into the local folklore,' said McMahon. 'I remember something about these things from what I heard as a boy.' He grabbed a packet of cigarettes and lit one, inhaling nervously. 'The first lot were piskies, I think; they don't do any harm. The second kind were spriggans, and their jokes are nothing to laugh at.'

Silence again. De Vere Ellis stared dully out of the open tent entrance toward Brown Willy. Then Browne-Smythe croaked with a harsh unpleasant voice, 'My God – I never dreamed for a moment...' He did not finish his sentence; it was unnecessary. Words were indeed useless. A nightmare had taken on flesh and blood and had assaulted them; talking could not calm their confusion.

McMahon remembered a flask of whisky included in his pack, and took it out. He handed it around, and the fierce liquor made them a little more sanguine.

'I feel quite mystified by all this,' said McMahon, somehow achieving reflective detachment. 'Is it possible for three people to dream the same nightmare at the same time?'

'There's no mystery,' said Browne-Smythe sourly. 'Those damned spriggans were tangible enough.'

'Oh, forget it!' snapped de Vere Ellis, savage now that for the first time in his life his logical beliefs were violently shaken. 'Forget the whole affair! Talk about it in the morning. I'm going to sleep if I can.'

'Happy dreams,' said Browne-Smythe, 'I shan't get any.'

'The blasted wind's going to stop us sleeping,' said McMahon with a yawn.

The wind was increasing power every minute. Soon it was seething and screaming across the summit, whipping in around their corner, snatching at the tent. Through it all they became aware of a dim stony creaking rising louder and faster, the sound of boulder on boulder. It was McMahon who realised what it was.

'It's the Logan Stone,' he said, 'rocking in the wind.'

It began to rain, though not on the tent. The heavy drops went over them, protected as they were by the Chapel rock, and splashed loudly on the boulders nearby. The Logan Stone oscillated yet more wildly, a gauge of the wind's violence; *clunk-clunk, clunk-clunk*, like a mad thing. The tent was illuminated in a lightning flash and they saw each other half-sitting up in bed with white faces. Then an enormous roll of thunder sounded immediately above them, rotating and exploding like some cosmic cannon; the rain redoubled and the windshrieks seemed to fade beside its dark drumming.

Browne-Smythe, whose bed was at the southern end of the tent nearest Brown Willy, put out his hand to secure the end flap more tightly. As he undid the knot the strings were plucked from his hand by the hurricane, and he had to half-crawl outside to regain them. Then wind entered, creasing the canvas and banging the lamps against the poles. Browne-Smythe was on his hands and knees in the doorway, they saw, when the lightning blinked again, but he was making no effort to close the flap.

'What's the matter?' yelled de Vere Ellis above the wind.

Browne-Smythe turned slowly, but as he was evidently speaking in his normal voice they could not hear him. He beckoned and then pointed to something. The other two crawled over to him.

Over the north slope of Brown Willy they could just distinguish a great jet figure against the fiercely dark sky. It was of human form, but the size of a giant; it was bending and stooping and appeared to throw up its arms to the clouds and down again, as though throwing something over its shoulder. They could not be sure. They lost the figure in darkness, thought they saw it again; then it was gone. What was it? Had they seen a real thing, or a mere trick played by the lightning and the black pregnant clouds?

'It might,' said McMahon very slowly when they had retreated into the tent. 'it might have been Tregeagle baling out Dozmary. The pool lies in that direction.'

'Giant ghosts now – Jesus!' muttered Browne-Smythe.

Insane fear and anger rushed through de Vere Ellis. Reason was playing him false tonight. He was bewildered, his brain nearly numb with helpless feelings. He wanted to scream, but with great effort overcame that longing, only to find that when he did so there were tears in his eyes, rolling down his face, and he had no power to stop them. It was at this moment that the other two decided to light a lamp for comfort, and hearing McMahon fumble with matches he

85

flung himself down on the nearest bed – Browne-Smythe's – and buried his face in the bedclothes.

'Hullo, old chap,' said Browne-Smythe stupidly when he saw him there. 'Anything up?'

De Vere Ellis said nothing for some moments, not trusting himself to speak without betraying emotion, and then made some explanation that Browne-Smythe in a normal time would have laughed at. But he too was confounded, and accepted the tale about hitting his head on the stony ground quite seriously. Against the voice of the wind McMahon had heard nothing of this, and having lit the lamp he began grumbling that there was very little oil left in it.

De Vere Ellis raised himself and shouted discordantly, 'You talk about the bloody lamp! What's the matter with you two; what d'you think this is, a boy scout's jaunt?'

No one replied for a minute, and then McMahon shouted back, 'You can't accept the supernatural; that's what's the matter with you. I've seen it: I believe and keep sane. You've seen it and you won't believe it: if you don't look out you'll go out of your mind!'

There was no time to reply to this. They heard a long piercing wail rising above the wind; it was a loud bass tortured voice from some distance away, like a trumpet gone mad and possessing the strength of ten trumpets. It was followed by a sound that could only be described as a laugh: a maniacal fiendish laugh, a great gloating chuckle out of the clouds. But they hardly had time to experience fresh fear at this, for the wind without the slightest warning veered round and flew in from the east in giant gusts. The Chapel rock was now no protection; with the rain sheeting down on the canvas came stones flung by the gale. Then a guy rope snapped and the tent collapsed on top of them.

There was only one thing to do. Thunderstruck as they were they managed to uproot the other pegs and drag the whole gear to the cave. It was merely shallow and left them half in, half out of the storm. They covered themselves up with blankets and the canvas.

Gathering stray items together McMahon found his big pipe and instinctively clutched hold of its familiar form.

Like a child clutching a teddy bear, he thought, and realising this, saw irony; but he could not smile. He thought of his peagreen scarf, de Vere Ellis' loud shirt, Browne-Smythe's moustache: the pop record and the cigarettes and the brandy – all futile vanities now strewn abandoned like children's playthings, or hugged but no longer comforting; and they themselves were suddenly no more than terrified children, afraid of what they did not understand.

They were now facing up the valley between Roughtor and Brown Willy, and saw without hindrance the last satanic stormy episode. There was a glaring yellow flash of lightning lasting several seconds, it seemed, which revealed that same dark figure towering against an inflamed sky and flying toward them down from the uplands. It was Tregeagle with his head in the clouds, whooping and screaming, running with thunderous footsteps. A hellhound pack pursued him with murderous baying.

Down between the two hills he came, bellowing out tormentedly. His great thighs were level with them as he passed, and his footsteps shook Roughtor itself so that loose stones fell down around them. His screams cut into them like knives, severing the roots of nerves and stabbing through the floors of sanity. At his heels those devildogs leaped, sabre fangs in cavernous jaws open for the kill. Their raucous throatings sawed the air, upward emanating like fists seizing, choking, with horror sickening those beholding. Night filled overpowering with sudden hellmighty voices, rock moor cloud abyss, two hills with terror yelling between them – were they, grovelling unbearably, the only things afraid?

Away westward the pack ran, echoes bellowing out among the tors even in the unabated wind, but diminishing as they went. De Vere Ellis was on his feet and ran round the Chapel rock to watch; he came back with face wet, but not with rain, and gibbered for the whisky. Browne-Smythe sat moaning unintelligibly like an idiot. McMahon himself, though quivering with shock, heart racing uncontrollably, did not dare think but searched for the flask. He found it under a pile of blankets and reached out to give it to de Vere Ellis.

Browne-Smythe snatched at it and they began to fight. McMahon did the only thing he could think of: he picked up a jagged stone weighing nearly half a hundredweight and snapped, 'I'll brain you both if you don't sit down and shut up!'

They calmed down a little. Browne-Smythe began his dull moaning again, looking around him piteously like a whipped cur.

'Listen,' said McMahon very firmly and calmly, 'there's only one thing to do – stay here at all costs.'

But then the baying and howling, which had never quite died away, became louder; Tregeagle and the savage yelping pack were returning. De Vere Ellis was on his feet in an instant, running away, scrambling frantically across the boulders. Browne-Smythe made as though to get up; McMahon leaned over and roared in his ear. 'Don't be a bloody fool! This is the only place were they can't hurt you!' He put his hand on his shoulder to prevent him rising.

But now they could hear the footsteps pounding. Browne-Smythe shrieked, flung himself sideways; tripped McMahon as he came at him and lashed out ferociously with his fist. He caught him on the jaw, and fled off across the rocks. McMahon fell, hit a boulder and lost consciousness.

✰✰✰

When he came around it was dawn and the sun, spinning crimson up over the moors, shone full into the Chapel cave. The wind was now merely a faint placid breeze, the clouds high, white and motionless. A lark was singing up among them, his ceaseless wings whirring.

This much McMahon observed sleepily; then realising he was cold, he moved to cover himself and found a sickening pain shooting through his head. He had ugly cuts and bruises on his temple.

He managed to wrap himself in blankets, and slept again for several hours. He was conscious from time to time of gathering warmth of the sun; and though he felt vaguely impressed by some recent event, he was too insensible to try and remember it, or ask himself what he was doing there so early in the morning on the hillside.

When he finally awoke his head was clear, the sun was high, and he remembered, not without shuddering, the adventures of the night. He got up, found a rock pool, bathed his face and wounds; donned an anorak belonging to Browne-Smythe, and went in search of the other two.

Obviously they had gone across to the north, with the object of reaching civilisation. Crossing the rocky backbone of Roughtor he saw the car was still there by the gate at the end of the road.

He found Browne-Smythe in a gorse clump very near the rumbling waterfall. He was asleep and snoring stertorously. When awakened he gave no sign of recognition, and said nothing; the only sound he made, at long intervals, was the same low moaning he had made in the night. He could not walk; his ankle was broken.

For about a fortnight Browne-Smythe suffered a complete loss of memory concerning himself and the events leading up to the morning he was found on the moor. Gradually his awareness of his past life and who he was returned, but he never recalled the events of that night on Roughtor; nor would he believe McMahon, who told him about them. Yet though he refused to accept the story, the cuts and weals on his back healed leaving ugly red scars which no doctor could ever satisfactorily explain.

Although he now owns the property left him by his father, McMahon does not often visit Cornwall. He lectures at a college in the Midlands, has a flat in London and is fond of travelling abroad.

De Vere Ellis was lost for two days, wandering the moors without any sense of bearing; he declared afterwards that he was convinced he was being led in circles by something, and marvelled that he had not been drowned in a bog. He has since taken up the study of parapsychology, and is in his way something of an authority on psychical research. One day, when he feels equal to the occasion, he may even go back to Roughtor; but whether to spend the night there in further research, he does not say.

THE HOMECOMING

For a man whose life over many years has been that of commerce and finance in great cities, the thought of returning home to one's birthplace in the Devon countryside can only be one of sweet allurement.

Lamerton Court, a mile or two outside Tavistock towards Dartmoor, has been in our family, the Mellors, for three centuries. It dates back to early Tudor times and was, in its original form, built by a de Courcy who owned tin workings and was a leading member of the Devon Stannary Parliament. If I had been born in such an age I should have had no need to go to London and the City to be successful.

Be that as it may, my career took me, in 1946 after my war service, into property and finance; I set up several companies and prospered, and somehow was always too busy – that is to say, there was always some sound business reason to prevent me, some deal to be clinched or customers to be wined and dined – to go home to Lamerton for Christmas.

My mother lived on there, leading a lonely life well into her seventies; my father died in 1960. The rest of the family were scattered, my only brother George, a sheep farmer in Australia, my sisters Doris and Joan both married and living upcountry, as we say. After Father's death there was only Great Aunt Alys, bright and sharp in her nineties, to keep Mother company, except of course when any of the family came home; as we all did from time to time, for a week or so.

Not since that year when I came out of the Army had we all been together at Christmas. In December 1972 letters and phone calls flew between us, for Mother was failing and it was her dearest wish to have us all around her, perhaps for the last time. George and his wife were flying home, Doris and Joan and their husbands were coming down from Manchester and Bristol with two or three of their children; and I was pressed to complete the family circle.

Of course I couldn't refuse. After all, I reflected, I could easily spare the time, having had a very good year and being faced with no pressing concerns. My latest bid on behalf of my shareholders to take over a chain of hotels had been accepted, and my group of companies would now be worth well over ten million pounds as a result. I turned down several invitations to parties and Christmas dinner, and phoned my latest lady friend (my wife and I had parted ten years before) to tell her I was called away on an urgent family matter – which, in view of Mother's poor health, was true.

'Brenda,' I said through my intercom, staring out at the drab London sky and fluorescent-lit South Bank buildings opposite across the river, 'could you help me with some Christmas shopping?'

'Certainly, Mr Mellor.' Brenda came in, smart, efficient, and middle-aged, with notebook and pencil ready: the best sort of secretary. No cute dolly birds for me.

'I'm giving you the rest of the afternoon to make a few well-chosen purchases for me to take down to Devon, Brenda. You'll have a much better idea of what to get than I would anyway.' I listed the whole family, from Aunt Alys and Mother down to the children (whose ages I could only vaguely guess; they must be growing up now), describing them all and their tastes as far as I could; and gave her fifty pounds and hoped it would be enough. 'And, if you'd be so good, book me a seat on the morning train to Tavistock the day after tomorrow.'

'That's Christmas Eve.'

'Ah. So it is.'

Usually I drove down to Lamerton in my Jaguar, especially enjoying the final part of the trip among the incomparable sweeping views of Dartmoor. But the day would be short, and I detested driving in the dark. Also I was developing an aversion to motorways (the M5 had now got as far as Taunton): all that tearing cut-throat haste to get somewhere half an hour earlier, at the risk of one's life. Yes, a good relaxing train journey, reminding me of years long past as I watched the landscape changing around me: that was the sensible thing, I was sure.

Brenda returned about four o'clock with the presents. A beautiful blue chiffon scarf for Aunt Alys, Chanel perfume for Mother, an Aran-knit pullover for George, some expensive hand-made chocolates for his wife Betty (whom I'd never met), and a well-chosen assortment of useful gifts for Doris and Joan and their husbands. The teenage children would share a large box of liqueur-filled chocolates between them, to make them feel grown up.

I was particularly busy the next day, putting my affairs in order at the office and my flat. I packed carefully, giving thought to what I might need for the week's stay at Lamerton; no doubt we would go out tramping across the Moor, so my heavy winter wear was necessary. I found time to go out to Swan and Edgar to buy a decent padded anorak with a waterproof outer skin, realising that my raincoat would no longer do. When Brenda gave me the train ticket and a Christmas card from herself I took little notice, merely wishing her a happy holiday and presenting her with the usual Christmas bonus. It wasn't until she had gone and I was left alone in the office, looking forward to a quiet meal at a restaurant while the rush-hour passed, that I glanced at the piece of printed green card which said *Return from Paddington to Plymouth*.

Rubbish, I thought. The route back home had always been from Waterloo, via Exeter, Okehampton and then down the valley to Tavistock. But of course British Rail had reorganised its regions since I last travelled by train, quite a number of years ago, so presumably... Brenda must have failed to notice the destination was wrong. Well, no doubt I could explain it at the other end. I'd have to get on the train at Paddington, but I would get out at Exeter and change for the Tavistock line. Quite simple; just like the old days.

At 10.50 the next morning I was on the train, drawing out past the dark and dusty warehouses and blocks of flats and offices in West London. Soon we looked down over Middlesex and Berkshire as we raced westward. As I lunched in the restaurant car I anticipated the Christmas we should have at Lamerton: roast turkey or goose with all the traditional trimmings, a rich dark pudding made by Mother herself (the only thing she would never let the cook do) from a very old family recipe, drenched in brandy and flaming on the table. And apples from our orchard, real old-time russets, Cox's Orange Pippin, Blenheims and a sharp Keswick to finish off dessert. Then carols round the piano (could Mother still play? Aunt Alys used to for many years, but her hands had become too arthritic). And the old tales would be told to a new generation, stories of family outings, Dartmoor characters and ghosts, of strange happenings on the farms and hills. Already I felt the growing glow and anticipation that accompanies every returning traveller long exiled from his home.

The train slid into Exeter St David's station. The cool voice of a girl came over the loudspeaker: 'The train now at Platform Four will call at Newton Abbott and Plymouth. Passengers for Dawlish and Teignmouth, please take the rear two coaches.'

I grabbed my luggage and got out. Taxi to Central Station, then, across the city. I wasn't going to be robbed of that romantic homecoming down the Tavy valley. I held out my ticket to the collector as I went through the barrier but in the crush of passengers he barely glanced at me as I said 'Tavistock,' and waved me through.

In the taxi I looked out at the late Christmas shoppers, the bright lights of the stores, the immense illuminated Christmas tree in the High Street near the Cathedral, and smiled to see the happiness around me. Then I got a great fright, for swerving across the road, apparently out of control, lights blazing and horn blaring, was a huge petrol tanker. 'My God!' I heard the driver cry, as he swung the wheel hard over to get out of its path.

This experience numbed my brain; after that it seemed I was travelling in a dream. I got to the Central station, found a train waiting, and, in the same traumatic state, jolted down to Okehampton, Lydford and Brentor. I was relieved to find they were still running steam trains on the line: *chuff-chuff, shudder-shudder, chuff-chuff, shudder-shudder*, sang the carriages over the rails. My schooldays passed again before me to the rhythm of the train, as I remembered my first excursion to Okehampton, to tramp the Moor and fish in the East Okement valley. The light was now failing fast, but there was still a pale cold yellow glow in the west; the great shadowy shapes of the west Dartmoor tors could be discerned above us to the east beyond Mary Tavy and Peter Tavy. Then at last we were pulling into Tavistock.

I expected the booking clerk, who was collecting the tickets, to question my destination, but he merely took mine, tore it in half and gave the return part back to me. Nothing to pay, anyway, I thought. Would there be a taxi here? Yes, there was one only waiting. 'Lamerton Court,' I said; the driver, an elderly man, touched his cap as they used to do in the good old days, and put my bags in the luggage space beside him. The car was a venerable Austin hackney carriage of the 1930s; I sank luxuriously into the ancient leather upholstery and stretched out my legs.

'Going to snow on the high moor tonight, they say.' The driver slid the glass partition back to speak.

'Shouldn't wonder at it,' I said, drawing my anorak about me tightly.

Lamerton Court is three miles outside Tavistock itself, and we rose steadily up towards Vixen and Heckwood Tors, which were among my earliest memories, etched on the skyline above the house. Stark, crazily twisting hawthorns and great grey naked beech trunks showed up in the lights of the car as we progressed; they made me feel at home, as though they were part of me and I part of them; as if they were my very bones and sinews. Small piles of frozen hail from the first fall of winter lay beside the ditches and on the hedges. We turned off the main Dartmoor road and went down the winding lane that led to our Jacobean-fronted house, and soon I saw its lights glimmering through the Scotch pines and copper beeches that surround it. The taxi drew up at the front door, which opened as I got out and paid the driver.

'Boy Robert,' said a quavering but joyful voice above me, and I looked up to see dear old Aunt Alys standing there on the steps. 'So here you are,' she said. 'Welcome home.'

A gust of wind blew icily across the grounds. 'You must go in, Auntie,' I said, 'or you'll catch your death.'

Inside a tall Christmas tree stood in the hall, draped with tinsel and winking with scores of tiny coloured lights. I took my presents in their gay wrappings from my bag and laid them under the tree, with the other gifts already there.

'You must be tired after your journey,' said Aunt Alys. 'Go on up to your room, it's all ready just as usual. I'll bring you up a hot drink.'

Suddenly I felt exhausted, though I couldn't understand why. Perhaps I had been overdoing things lately; certainly I had not been sleeping too well at night. I yawned and dragged my luggage up to the room on the first floor I had occupied from the age of three years until I grew up. I took off my anorak and jacket, lay out on the bed and fell immediately asleep, before the drink was brought up.

When I awoke it was about seven o'clock. They would all be downstairs waiting for me to join them at dinner. I washed, put on a clean shirt, changed into my lounge suit and went down. Yes; they were all there around the huge log fire, some with drinks in their hands, but something was wrong, I sensed; they seemed subdued. Mother, thin and frail, was conversing in low tones with George, whilst Betty sat talking to my two sisters on the sofa. Over by the window their husbands watched, saying very little. Even the youngsters, Jennifer and Philip and Robin, were quiet.

'Ah well,' I heard, 'it was only to be expected at her age. She would have wanted to see Robert before she went, though.'

'It doesn't look as if he's going to be here in time for dinner,' Doris said. 'The train must have been delayed.'

At this point I came into the room, but no one greeted me. 'Hullo, mother. Good to see you George,' I said, but they didn't even turn their heads. I stood there staring at them all as the dinner gong sounded and George took Mother in, followed by the others. I went after them into the dining room, and saw eleven places laid at the table. Around the walls were the old portraits I knew so well, of Mellors going back centuries; the last painting was of my grandfather, Sir

Jonathan, a venerable old man who died when I was ten. My father and his brother Albert were there too, though their portraits were large framed photos from the 1940s. Just as I was about to sit down at the empty eleventh place, obviously laid for me, there was the sound of a telephone ringing, and then a servant appeared in an agitated manner. 'Oh Madam, there's been an accident; will you answer the phone?'

'I'll go.' George went out into the hall where the phone was, and I heard him say, 'In Exeter? How... Oh my God!... I see. Well, thank you; we'll come as soon as we can.' He came back, his faced drained of colour.

'It's Robert. He's been killed in a road accident. A runaway lorry in Exeter crushed the taxi he was in. Someone has to go up and identify the body...'

Mother broke down into tears. I tried to console her, tugging her arm. 'It isn't true, Mother, look, look, I'm here...' But there was no contact, no response.

'What was he doing in a taxi?' Joan said puzzledly.

'They're not sure,' George told her, 'but it seems he was going from St David's station to the Central.'

'He must have forgotten there aren't any trains from Exeter Central to Tavistock now,' Doris said. 'The lines were taken up ten years ago.'

'No, no!' I shouted. 'I was on that train. Look, I'm here! I got to Tavistock, I did, I arrived!'

Someone jogged my elbow. It was my dear Aunt Alys, who put her finger to her lips and let me gently out of the room as the others tried to comfort Mother, sobbing in her grief.

'Come along now, Boy Robert,' said my Aunt. 'We've got some walking to do, you and I, but we'll be meeting your father, and Uncle Albert, your grandfather all the family who have gone on before us.'

I followed her out of the room. As we passed the Christmas tree in the hall I noticed that my presents were no longer there. Outside the north-east wind moaned in the pines, bringing the first few flakes of snow, but I didn't feel its impact on my coatless form. We walked on in that strange dreamlike journey, out across the Moor, past the gaunt glimmering rock piles on Great Mis Tor, by Wistman's Wood the gushing torrents of the upper Dart valley; past Princetown and the blazing lights of the Prison, over towards Dartmeet, Hexworthy and Ashburton; on and on through the whirling snow, tirelessly walking into the night...

A SKELETON IN THE CUPBOARD

On a dour March day in the late 1970s, Terence P. Conrad was marooned in a damp insanitary cottage on the edge of Bodmin Moor, bad-temperedly struggling to create something in verse. Until lately book reviewer on the left-wing intellectual Sunday Subverser, Terence had been diagnosed as having a peptic ulcer in an advanced stage. Deciding that it was high time to quit the pressures of city life and to indulge at last his unfulfilled creative instincts, he and his wife Hilda had removed to the parish of St Breward.

Now he sat glowering at the innocent piece of paper in his typewriter. Through the narrow window, past the bulging, heavily-papered cob wall, he could see the long curves of the moor rising and falling towards bleak hills with outlandish names like Brown Gelly, Hantergantick, Rough Tor and Garrow Tor. These he viewed with considerable distaste. Again he considered the few lines he had typed, and scowled more darkly. Poetry, to Terence, had to be *committed*: in other words, sociologically and politically meaningful. He recognised no other sort. But having written these words in a state of euphoric hatred the previous night, after several whiskies to console himself for the inhospitable country in which he found himself, he was now reduced to wondering what on earth he had intended by them.

> The bloody leaves of war rain down:
> Brainlust of megalomaniac energies
> Release our foredoomed fate.
> Empty cans and orange peel, ice-cream cartons,
> Tattered bags of chips, portend our summer Hells...

He got up and walked about the cramped living room in an agony of disappointment. He daren't show Hilda this; she would only laugh and tell him to read Ezra Pound. (That Fascist!) He went into the kitchen and gazed out over the moor in the other direction, down towards Tintagel and Boscastle. There lay the supposed King Arthur country, where all was devoted to the glory of that fictitious monarch: King Arthur's Tea Rooms, the Camelot petrol station, King Arthur's Hall with fake Round Table, and the ruined medieval castle on the cliffs where the non-king had supposedly reigned. Terence sniffed, then bent down to examine something he noticed under the sink.

He had to admit he'd never seen such multi-coloured and obscenely-shaped fungi before; if they hadn't had the staggering effrontery to grow there (overnight, he was sure, not having seen them when he made himself some coffee after penning those ineffable lines), he would have removed them immediately and thrown them out of doors. But really, they were something of a marvel, and Hilda ought to see them before he took such action. A slow and bitter smile spread over his narrow features; he stroked his greying goatee beard in delicious anticipation. Yes: he would certainly save them for Hilda.

On re-entering the living room he passed his wife's latest model sculpture, sitting primly on the table by the wall, at odds with all else about it. Imitation Barbara Hepworth, he thought, dismissing the involuted curves and gaps with brief contempt. Then he took the paper out of the typewriter, tore it into small pieces and threw them into the empty grate. He warmed his hands at the oil heater they had bought in Camelford, and shuddered to think what a long and rocky road he had to travel before he could call himself a great poet. But he mustn't be downhearted. A tot of whisky, a cigarette, and a fresh start. The first line wasn't all that bad, after all: he'd keep that and build on it. 'The bloody leaves of war rain down...' he said aloud. No: 'In bloody battalions the leaves of war rain down.' Better. But what next? He felt something emerging from the depths of his jaundiced mind, took up a fresh sheet of paper and prepared to type; but then a small superannuated car was heard ascending the hill and drawing up in the lane outside. Blast. Hilda always managed to time her entrances for the maximum destructive effect.

'Hullo; still at it?' his wife said cheerfully, entering with two loaded shopping baskets. An unproductive remark, to say the least, thought Terence.

'You could put it that way; though I wouldn't.' He began to type, hoping she would take the hint.

Not Hilda. 'Tough going eh?' She put down her bags and sat down.

Terence grunted. 'Like batting your head against a brick wall – nice when you leave off,' he said. He got up, drew deeply on his cigarette, and stared out of the window.

'I got all I could from the Cash and Carry,' Hilda was saying. 'Couldn't afford a joint for the weekend, though. D'you mind?'

'Don't talk to me about food, please, Hilda.'

'Of course,' she went on, 'it's no doubt a very healthy experience, this, for us. Fifty pounds a week on Social Security is still luxury compared to what those poor devils in Africa and Asia are getting...'

This appeal to his basic socialism struck no sparks from Terence. 'They could have all my cornflakes and fish-fingers, if only I could have electric light,' he said.

Hilda sighed; she had heard all this before. If you take a cottage on the moor you must be prepared to do without some things; it was part of the charm of the place, in her view. She was now examining her sculpture: picking up a lump of clay she thumbed in a piece or two. 'Of course, after my exhibition we should be able to move into a decent winter let – maybe a nice bungalow on the coast.' She was due to put on a show at St. Ives in September: five months away.

'If you sell anything,' sniffed Terence. 'Well, I suppose you can always switch to Cornish garden piskies – they're always in demand, it seems.'

Wounded, Hilda turned her deep psychic grey eyes on him. 'Now really, Terence. I thought this little place would inspire you. If I can work here, why can't you? All this nature... the wild life... the moors outside... and you must admit, the cottage has real atmosphere.'

Terence stubbed out his cigarette venomously. 'Draughts in the floorboards, wind in the chimney, mildew on the

100

walls and no mod. cons.' He stared at the wallpaper over the fireplace, where damp patches were bringing out large whitish-grey patches of mould. No doubt a good fire in the chimney would cure that, but Terence hadn't retired to Cornwall to chop wood or stoke fires.

'As far as I can see, there's only one thing to worry about,' Hilda was saying. She went across to the door which led off from the living room: it had been a kind of storeroom or dairy, they imagined, for it had a stone-flagged floor and only one very small window. It was cold and dark inside, and they had no occasion to use it. But something odd, something distinctly disturbing, had been going on in there during the last day or two. There was little which one could define, or indeed wish to admit; and neither of them so far had done more than hint vaguely to each other that all was possibly not quite as well as it might be inside that unused room.

Hilda was now at the door. 'I thought I heard...' she said. Her voice trailed away as she strained to listen.

'What did you hear?'

'I don't know exactly... just something...'

Terence said nothing, but began to sort through his notes again.

'Did you hear anything while I was out?' she asked.

'What should I hear?'

'I'm sure I...'

And then she distinctly heard it. A note of medium pitch, like a slate or chimney pot being rapped, quite deliberately: but it was neither of stone nor ceramic origin. 'There! I knew there was something,' she said.

Terence, who had heard it and not heard it (which is to say that the sounds without doubt impinged on his eardrums, but that he immediately closed his mind to any possible mysterious origin), said firmly, 'You're just imagining things again, Hilda. You're up to your old psychic tricks again. Because we're in Cornwall and it's supposed to be a haunted sort of place, we have to have noises. I've no doubt they're all perfectly natural and explicable.'

101

'Well, explain that one.'

'What was it like?'

'Difficult to say really. I don't quite know...' The sardonic twist to Terence's mouth stung her into attempting a description. 'Like something hollow being hit or dropped.'

'Probably the rafter creaking again. The wind's rising, I think.'

Hilda was examining the mildew on the wall. 'This is certainly getting worse,' she said. 'Enough to put one off one's food.'

'Did you see the agent about it?'

'I called at the office but he wasn't in. I left a complaint and the girls said he'd call.' She began to wipe off the mould with a tissue.

'Then why not leave it for him to see?'

'I'm simply not going to... live for another hour... in such...'

'A place of charm and seclusion?' suggested Terence.

'. . . Slum conditions for anyone. There – at least it does come off.' She regarded the grey streaks left with a frown.

'When you've finished doing that, have a go at the kitchen,' he said maliciously.

'What's wrong with the kitchen?'

'Have a look under the sink.'

After giving him a blank look, Hilda marched into the kitchen; a quiet smile of satisfaction emerged on Terence's waspish features as he heard her scream in brief outrage. Then she came back actually holding those prize specimens of fungi, closely examining them.

'Good God, Hilda, did you have to pick them?'

'I certainly couldn't do any cooking with these in there. But they're rather fascinating in a way – when you really look at them.' She found an empty jam jar and arranged them in it delicately. 'Such suggestive domed shapes – rather phallic, I suppose.'

'Disgustingly so. Hey – ' as Hilda placed the jar on the table beside his typewriter and stood back to view them, 'get them out before I throw 'em out. They stink.' He wrinkled his nose.

102

But she took no notice. Terence lit another cigarette. The toadstools sat there, glowing orange and purple, quietly fluorescent in the shadowy room. Outside, the day was still heavy with lowering cloud-drifts, and the narrow cottage windows admitted little light. Terence got up, fiddled with the Victorian oil lamp (Hilda had bought it from an antique shop in Wadebridge for what he considered a grossly inflated price), and finally got it to light up.

'I think,' Hilda said, 'there's something there I can use. Yes. A bas-relief, possibly; or a large group based on their forms...' She took up her pad and pencil and began rapidly sketching the fungi. 'About five feet high,' she added.

'Good God. Can't imagine anybody wanted to buy that,' Terence muttered.

But she was now totally absorbed in her drawing, holding up her pencil from time to time and estimating the proportions of the fungi. So he took advantage of the welcome silence to concentrate on his poem, and began it again. Other words now appeared on the virgin paper.

In bloody battalions the leaves of war rain down;
Nadir contortions of limbs and entrails shout silence,
Yell dumb agonies:
Our perihelion reached whilst babes are sacrificed;
Appease the Gods, our ancestors believed, and we
Do no less by our taxes and our toil, whereby
The juggernauts grow fat and greedy on our ignorance...

Well, he thought, it's different. It may even be better. He'd go over it tomorrow and see how it struck him – whether with a blinding flash or a dull thud. He still resisted the impulse to ask Hilda what she thought: she could be unnecessarily scathing about his creative efforts. Once she had called his verse a pale imitation of Stephen Spender, tarted up with a few contemporary references. For most of their married life she had been an ardent Marxist like himself, but lately she had defected. She had gone through a whole series of conversions and convolutions, from Terence's point of view, having now tried everything from Fabianism to Trotskyism and fallen out with the whole socialistic ethos because it wouldn't fit in with her eccentricities. Now she was on Zen Buddhism and Extra Sensory Perception; she'd finish up a Catholic at this rate, in his view, and they'd have to part. Whatever failings Terence himself had, inconsistency was not one of them: he had been converted to materialist Marxist-Leninism in early adolescence and now, forty-five years later, having weathered the age of Stalin, the years of Kruschev, the suppression of Czechoslovakia, Hungary and Poland, he was all the more confirmed in his principles.

They worked in parallel concentrations for nearly twenty minutes. Terence began to believe that the grand design of his poem was at last emerging. He saw it in six sections, with interposed satirical lyrics: a feeling rose in his tight narrow chest (35 inches around) that here would be something to compare with the works of his great heroes, the revolutionary poets Blok and Lorca and Myakovsky and Yevtushenko. Then it happened again.

'There!' Hilda nearly dropped her sketch pad. 'Listen! You *must* have heard it that time.'

And he had, though it was the last thing he would have admitted. What the hell did it matter, anyway? Hilda was at the door leading to the inner room, and now summoned up enough courage to open it and peep inside. 'I believe,' she said, 'it came from *that cupboard.*'

That cupboard was certainly an impressive piece of furniture – large enough to store a whole sheep, a side of beef, or a man, inside it. The doors were immensely heavy, with medieval carvings on them. It was massive and practically immovable, and had no doubt been undisturbed for centuries. There had been absolutely nothing in it, except dust and a few bleached and harmless bones, which surely couldn't have had anything to do with the noise.

'Probably,' Terence said with a certain enjoyment, 'it's a poltergeist.'

'Do you really think so?' said Hilda. 'I thought that the spirits in this part of the world were rather gentle and intimate – more like one of the family, I've heard.'

Terence snorted. 'Definitely: every home should have

one.' He fitted another sheet of paper into his typewriter. He poised his fingers to begin again when there was a knock on the door, which caused him to curse again.

Hilda got up to answer it, and met a middle-aged, tall, boney, sharp-faced woman entering as if she too lived there. 'Oh, I hope you good people wun't mind me coming in on you like this without a word of warning,' this person said with propitiating smile and a broad North Cornish accent. Her eyes darted about the room like needles. 'Only you see, I'm your nearest neighbour, my dears – I live just across the field there, and I've always got on well with the other parties who've taken this little place – not that many of 'em have stayed long...'

'I don't doubt that,' muttered Terence.

'Now if you should want any eggs, or a pint or two of goats' milk...'

'Goats' milk?' echoed Hilda.

'Very nourishing, so they reckon. It've got a higher protein yield than cow's milk, you know. I got free range hens, too. Large or standard sizes, bantam's eggs, and cracked ones for cooking.'

'Well, I shall be glad to have some eggs, Mrs... er...'

'Tresize. Janey Tresize.' She smiled at them, a peculiarly challenging wizened smile, as she stood there in her apron, and on her grey head a round black hat of immense age, with a long hat pin. 'Course, y'knaw, us Cornish are s'posed to be so stand-offish with you upcountry people. So I thought I better be neighbourly and come over right away to wance and tell 'ee tid'n true. If there's anything I can help 'ee with, just holler out: I'm inside spitting distance, as you might say.' The cottage she lived in, a low building with a bowed lichened slate roof, was partly hidden by twisted thorn trees stretching north-east before the prevailing wind: Terence and Hilda hadn't considered that anyone might actually inhabit it.

'Course,' continued the indomitable flow of local views and information, 'I'm all on me own now, since me old man died. He was killed in a accident, down to the china clay works last year.'

105

Feeling obliged to react to this apparent plea for sympathy, Hilda said, 'Oh, I'm sorry to hear that...'

But Janey evidently delighted in telling the story. 'Yes, 'e got caught in a conveyor belt and tipped out with ten ton o' gravel. Poor Fred...' she sighed pleasurably. 'Still, he wad'n no great loss to me, really. Always out awver the pub in the evenings; never did a hand's turn round the house. And they did give me a nice present o' money by way o' compensation.'

'Neglect on the company's part?' asked Hilda. Terence, looking steadfastly out of the window, began to listen.

'Well, that's what the union said. But he was a useless article, my Fred. Always putting his big foot in it – and that's how he met his Maker, dragged up the clay tip by his bootlaces. Still, mustn't brood over the past, must I?' Janey gave a final sigh of satisfaction and turned to view Hilda's sculpture. 'Ullo, then: I see you'm a artist.'

'Yes. I do sculptures, mainly.'

Janey went nearer and bent over to consider the strange shape and its abstractions.

'Oh, I see.' It was obvious that she didn't. 'Whass this going to be, then?'

'It doesn't actually represent anything. Certain motifs are drawn from the landscape around here – the stones on the moor and their weather-worn shapes.' Terence's lips curled and he closed his eyes.

'You mean, 'tid'n goin' to *be* anything?'

'Not in that way. The thing is, the inter-relationship of the shapes and the spaces between them.'

Terence gave a half-muffled snort and turned it into a cough. He fumbled for another cigarette.

'Mmm...' Janey stood back, considering the clay shape critically. 'Course, I s'pose you could always use it for a umbrella stand...' She lost interest in it and turned her sharp questing eyes on to Terence's table. 'If tid'n rude of me, what do your husband do?'

Hilda saw the spasm of acute annoyance pass across Terence's face, and blithely said, 'Actually he's a literary

106

critic: he writes for the Sunday Subverser. At present, though, he's working on a book of verse.'

Terence closed his eyes, praying that Mrs. Tresize had little acquaintance and less interest in such things. But the pattern of the lady's curiosity was becoming only too clear.

'Ah, thass nice. You knaw, I'm very fond of a bit o' poetry meself.'

'You are, Mrs. Trevice?' Terence heard Hilda say with some surprise.

'Tresize. But I'm Janey to me friends.'

'Well... Janey, then.'

'Oh yes,' said Janey firmly. 'Last winter, down to Boswurgey W.I., we done a whole course on modern poets. I some enjoyed it. We done Gerald Manley Hopkins, William Butlin Yeats, T.B. Eliot and Dielan Thomas.'

Terence shuddered visibly, then with an effort controlled and calmed himself. He had a shrewd notion of what this was leading to.

'Did you really? You hear that, Terence?' said Hilda, amused, well knowing that Janey could not have chosen four poets more abhorrent to him.

'Ah, 'twas handsome stuff, most of it,' Janey continued. 'Wonderful words, though to tell 'ee the truth I never really found out what half of 'em mean.'

'You're not alone in that,' muttered Terence. Weavers of word patterns, musicians of literature, glorifiers of sound: all vain and pompous obscurers of the political truths he himself sought. But it appeared that Janey had found such stuff of some therapeutic value.

'That course helped me a brave lot after my Fred passed up.' She edged nearer to Terence, peering at this typewriter and sheets of paper. ''Tis great comfort, a bit o' poetry, don't 'ee agree?' He found himself solicited by the ingenuous eyes behind her spectacles.

For the sake of peace, a lesser man might have agreed. Not Terence. He looked at Janey and said with the cool precision of a lawyer demolishing an opponent's case, 'To be brutally

107

honest, I don't find it comforting; quite the reverse. I don't indulge in that kind of overblown hot-house stuff myself.'

Janey, however, wasn't easy to demolish. Riding this like a skilful boxer taking an obvious punch, she said, 'Oh, but I should dearly love to hear one of yours, then – if you'd be so kind.'

'I'm afraid,' said Hilda hastily, sensing disaster, 'he hasn't quite finished them yet...'

'Quite all right, Hilda.' Terence was ready for the kill. A viciously joyful anticipation rose in him as he searched among his papers and found a poem he had written last week: a vision of all the futile wars of mankind, or so he believed. Standing up and holding it before him he paused to gain effect, and with the eyes of both women on him – Janey ready to applaud, Hilda wary and dubious – he recited in grating staccato tones:

> Entrenched bacteria emit the poisoned clouds,
> Rat-snuffled vomit as the gangrene mounts
> On all our past deceits and prides beslimed
> By protozoa of existence. O *Zeitgeist und Ego,*
> *Warum*? What spake Abelard,
> Rutting in the truffles of her lust
> Who trimmed his loins with love's philosophy?'

He sat down and folded his arms, watching Janey. There was considerable silence; expressions of bafflement, doubt and suspicion of being hoaxed, flickered across her face. Finally she said slowly, 'Yes... well, 'tid'n so pretty a piece as Dielan would write; though I'm sure 'tis very sincere.' She paused and delivered her most trenchant criticism. 'I don't b'lieve I heard any rhymes in it, did I?' She made a move towards the door, to Terence's gratification. 'Well, I better be going... I got a yeasty caake in me oven... I'll bring 'ee over some eggs later on...'

But Hilda had been thinking. 'Oh before you go, Janey... I was just wondering...'

With a pointed lack of courtesy Terence began to type. Hilda moved to the door with Janey. 'No doubt you've lived here for some time?' she asked.

'All me life, and me people fer generations before me.'

'Ah: then no doubt you'd have heard any reports of supernatural phenomena connected with this cottage?'

'Supernatural...?' Janey seemed at a loss, but only momentarily. 'Do 'ee mean ghosts an' things? Well now...' A look of furtive cunning stole upon her. The sharp nose and jutting chin with a few grey hairs on it came close to Hilda's face. 'Now I may have heard mention... not that you could call it anything definite, you understand... why, have you heard anything?'

'As a matter of fact,' said Hilda solemnly, 'we have.'

Janey lowered her voice. 'What have 'ee heard?'

'Noises!'

'Ah!' The black piercing eyes held Hilda in acute examination. 'What sort?'

'Well... sort of... *clonking* sounds.'

Their heads close together, the two women were unaware that Terence had stopped typing and was now sidling suspiciously towards them, listening hard.

'*Clonking?*'

'And we've – found something.'

Janey drew in her breath sharply. 'Have 'ee now! An' what was it?'

'Never mind!' Terence shouted, immediately behind her. 'None of your confounded business, Mrs. Trefoil.'

Drawing herself up haughtily – suddenly straightened up she seemed considerably taller than he was, almost towering over him – Janey said with disdain, 'Tresize, if you plaise. All right mister – I can see when me presence ed'n appreciated. I'm going, don't 'ee worry – '

'Oh, take no notice of him,' said Hilda, annoyed at Terence's tactics. She turned the full force of her own contempt upon him. 'He's just a constipated versifier. Word-bound, that's his trouble.'

Finally defeated, Terence went back to his table and returned to staring sulkily out of the window at the moor, already darkening at four o'clock. The clouds were blacker and surlier than ever, matching his mood precisely.

'I still want the eggs, Janey,' he heard Hilda say placatingly. Wherever they lived, Hilda always did her utmost to maintain cordial relations with neighbours.

'All right, you shall have 'em, missus,' said Janey. She went out. Hilda heard her complaining to herself, 'I'm sure I don't knaw what to make o' some of these arty people that come down here from England; 'tis enough to make you wonder why they d' bother to come, they'm so dissatisfied with it all when they get here...' Outside she turned, regarded the cottage with a baleful glare, and muttered something under her breath, as if it were a curse or an incantation. Screwing up her eyes she nodded five times fiercely at the back door, with its peeling paint and rotting bottom edges; and marched away, as if consigning the place and its occupants to an unknown and terrible perdition.

Inside Hilda was saying, ' I knew it! She's definitely heard something. If you hadn't interrupted she'd have told me. There's some mystery connected with the place – I wondered how we got it so cheap.'

'I should have thought,' said Terence wearily, making desultory notes on his sheets, 'that a genuine ghost or two on the premises would have trebled the rent.'

Hilda sat down, preoccupied again with the occult. 'I do wish you'd stop scoffing for one moment and consider the whole pattern of events,' she said. 'What sort of poet do you call yourself? Not an ounce of E.S.P. in you. Walter de la Mare and D.H. Lawrence – now there were two real poets. And Cornwall scared them both stiff – a haunted land, they said, and got out.'

'Can't say I blame them,' Terence said. 'You're just bloody determined to find something weird to justify your choice of the dreariest, most God-forsaken place in the British Isles.'

They were now at opposite poles of the human mind, as only too often occurred: Terence doggedly, malevolently materialistic, Hilda bravely, long-sufferingly psychic. She regarded him with pity and irritation; then said suddenly, 'You did hear it, though, didn't you?'

'No I didn't,' he said automatically. 'Hear what?'

'I know you did, though of course you won't admit it.

Well, I realise I'm hypersensitive, but I hear it all the time. And not only hear, but feel it. Here.' She placed her hand just below her bosom.

'You're quite sure,' Terence said, 'you're not pregnant?'

Hilda treated this cheap sneer with the contempt it deserved. 'No thanks to you if I were.' They had had separate beds for over four years now – she assumed he wasn't interested in, or wasn't capable of, the sexual aspects of their marriage; though they never actually discussed such things. 'I know that what I feel, and hear, are definitely connected with... *them*.' She nodded towards the inner room.

Terence barely ceased scribbling to answer indifferently, 'Why not get rid of them, if they bother you?'

'Get rid of them?'

'Quite simple, you know. I'll bury them down in the garden, or out on the moor, shall I?'

Hilda could hardly believe he was serious; that he wasn't, as usual, leading her on for his own amusement. Yet it was a suggestion worth considering, she felt.

'Somebody would see you,' she said, after a moment or two. 'Janey Tresize is probably over there watching every move we make.'

'I'll do it after dark, then.'

Hilda considered. 'No...' she decided reluctantly. 'Somehow I sense it wouldn't be right. They must be treated with respect... we're not competent to handle such things...'

'Oh, very well,' Terence said, his impatience breaking through again. 'Have it your own way. Now, d'you think I could have a few minutes in peace to get on with this?'

She sat brooding, but allowed him to write for almost two minutes. He was finding his ideas now falling into place. Yes: the vision of his masterpiece was definitely emerging. Belief in himself, a rare and precious asset, was gradually but surely being rediscovered.

'Perhaps,' said Hilda then, 'we ought to tell the police.'

Inside Terence a terrible black rage exploded, or rather imploded: his mind and body seemed to crumple under the impact of this treacherous suggestion. After twelve years of life with his revolutionary principles, Hilda still thought like a chattelled pre-suffragette female. 'If that isn't a typically fascist-bourgois suggestion of yours!' he heard his voice croak. 'That's it, call in the fuzz. What the hell good d'you think they'd do? It would only bring us publicity..'

'Perhaps,' Hilda said, 'we could do with some of that. The telly people might come down and film us. I can see it now. "Hilda Aldren, the sculptor, and Terence Conrad, the author and reviewer, have made an intriguing discovery in an old Cornish cottage..."' 'Quite a feature, eh?'

By God,' said Terence with slow-burning despair, 'I believe you really would.'

'Would what?'

'Tell them. Sell out to decadent capitalism, just to get your name mentioned on the box. Look, Hilda, I have come to this remote and wretched place for peace and solitude, and I will have peace and solitude if I have to shoot you and everyone else within a radius of three miles.' He took up his pen again and poised it over the paper.

Hilda sighed. 'I suppose you're right. It would be a betrayal of all our principles... though sometimes I feel we have too many of those for our own comfort. But...' she went to the inner door and listened. 'I still feel... that something should be done...'

At which point there were two more noises, a double clonk so loud and clear it seemed to her to come from the other side of the door: it was so insistent, so unavoidable that Terence himself was startled. He closed his eyes in despondency: how on earth could he write his masterpiece with Hilda's neuroticism and a background of annoying inexplicable sounds?

Hilda was no coward, morally or physically. 'There! Two this time. I'm going to find out once and for all.' She stepped up bravely and flung the door open.

Inside the room was bare and silent. She went in slowly, looking about her. It was a watchful silence, she decided: something in there was waiting, observing her. She closed the door quietly and came out.

'I didn't tell you this, Terence – I don't know why – but

112

last night I had another look inside that cupboard. It seemed to me – of course it was dark – that they weren't just there in a heap any old how, as they were before. They were... in a sort of arrangement.'

Terence gave up, let his pen fall, and screwed up his notes in an agony of rage and chagrin. Then hastily he began unscrewing and smoothing them out.

'Did you hear what I said?'

'Yes, yes! I heard. All right – let's hear it – what sort of arrangement?'

'Like a body. In fact, a skeleton. As if somebody had been trying to piece them all together.' An idea came to her. She looked at him accusingly. 'It wasn't you, by any chance, was it?'

Terence held his head in his hands. Behind his closed eyes red and violet clouds quaked and intermingled: they were pierced through by brilliant star effects, as he compressed his eyelids to keep back tears of baffled anger. His iron-bound code of life would never permit his own wife to see him reduced to weeping. He mastered himself with a gulp like a pigeon being strangled, and said as calmly as he could manage, 'No. It wasn't me. Why on earth do you suppose I should play such a prank?'

'I don't know why – unless to make fun of me.'

He got up and strode restlessly about. 'Hilda, it's time you realised I really am not interested in your pile of... mouldy old bones. Let the dead bury the dead, as...' he tried to remember who had said that, but failed '. . . as somebody so aptly put it.'

'I suppose, then, you think they've moved by themselves? Nobody's been in there but me – unless it was you.'

Terence pounded his fists on the table in an ineffectual spasm of frustration. The typewriter jumped and the toadstools fell off onto the floor. 'It's no good!' he shouted. 'We shall have to go back. I can't stand this – let's get back to town – to civilisation – perhaps then you'll become a reasonably well-balanced member of society again!'

Hilda let him calm down a little before saying, in her most

implacable tone, 'Terence: I dare you to go in and look at them.'

'Why the hell should I?'

'Just to prove that I'm not neurotic, insane, or subject to hallucinations.'

'I'm not interested. I just want to...'

'You're afraid to, in case I'm right. You want to go on sneering at my sensitivities, don't you?'

'Oh, blast your sensitivities!' He picked up the toadstools and hurled them into the fireplace, where they disintegrated into pulp. 'Oh... very well, if it'll make you any happier...'

He marched to the door, opened it with a wrench, and went in. He went over to the cupboard and opened it. What he saw there made him pause for several seconds. Hilda, watching from the doorway, was taken aback to see him slam the cupboard door and exit from the stone-flagged room in considerable haste. He almost ran to his table, then collected the remnants of his dignity together, and sat down slowly and thoughtfully.

'Well?' asked Hilda.

'You're... right.' It cost him a great deal of effort to say it. 'They have moved.'

'Didn't I tell you?'

'In fact,' said Terence pondering deeply, 'They've joined up.'

Hilda gave a little scream. 'What?'

'They are actually now a complete skeleton. All connected.'

'Con...nected?' stammered Hilda. 'B-but how...?'

'And,' said Terence, with an irritatingly mysterious smile, 'sitting in a semi-erect posture.'

'Oh my God!' Hilda sat down suddenly, staring at the door.

Terence had already divined the explanation. What other could there be? She must think him an idiot to be taken in for a moment by such a trick – though it was clever, he admitted to himself: she had devised this way to shake him out of his obdurate materialist philosophy. She now sat

114

twisting her handkerchief around her knuckles, frowning deeply: there was no need to keep up the act any longer, he thought. 'Now don't lay it on too thickly, Hilda. It's quite obvious, your little plan, to make me believe in your paraphysical hotchpotch of theories – or was it to interrupt my work? Anyway, my dear, I'm sorry to inform you that I'm not particularly impressed. And you will not prevent me from achieving my aim.' He smoothed out the crinkled sheets of paper containing his notes, viewing them with satisfaction. 'I am now in process of crystallising my attitude to the whole politico-economic development of the last fifty years... I shall begin work on the section tomorrow – or even this evening, if we can ignore these silly contretemps.'

But Hilda wasn't listening. She had extracted a book from one of the orange boxes in which they had stored their personal things: a work on psychic research. 'I had absolutely no idea... This is something new in my experience of the occult...' She turned the pages, searching for references. 'I must consult the S.P.R....'

Terence smiled sadly. But what did it matter? He fitted a virgin sheet of paper to the typewriter and immediately ravished it with an idea for a title that had suddenly come to him. 'The Price of Progress.' He sat back and considered it. Not bad. They'd soon see they had a new thinker of insight and vision to contend with. He knew now, with a quiet confident certainty, that here was his own unique contribution to the world of literature and politics. After all, what in fact had he achieved until now? A couple of slim travel books – *Across Herzogovina on a Bicycle* and *In the Footsteps of Goya* – his review column in the Subverser, an occasional article for one of the weekend glossies on some side-aspect of writing; and a feature for Playboy on Transvestism in fourteenth century Verona (sandwiched, he remembered with a shudder, between a nude with a forty-inch bust on one page and Danny La Rue on the next). Ah, but now, at last, the prospect was quite different. And Hilda was definitely not going to foul it all up with her parapsychological nonsense. He began a sub-heading: 'Notes towards a definition of economic-cultural self-realisation...'

A vehicle drew up outside. Looking out Terence saw a large modern estate car in the lane, and pounded his table again in silent, almost weeping frustration. Might as well try to write in the middle of Piccadilly Circus, he cursed to himself.

The car door slammed and heavy footsteps approached the outer door, followed by several firm knocks. Hilda went to open it; Terence heard a man's voice. Then she ushered in a large man in a tweed jacket and cavalry twill trousers. 'Mr. Menhennit, the agent.'

'Good afternoon, sir,' said this gentleman cheerfully. He spoke in a slow North Cornish accent, with booming vowels and richly rolled r's. 'Now I believe there was something troubling you here?'

Sunk in despondency, Terence closed his eyes and hoped this unwelcome presence would simply go away.

But Hilda was girding herself for battle. 'We certainly have. It's the whole condition of the cottage, really: it's not at all what we were led to expect.'

'Condition?' Menhennit looked about him, and sniffed. 'Hm... well, there is a sort of dead smell... but then you've got all your windows closed, you know.' He looked more closely at the streaked wall, beslimed with the remains of the mould, and touched it with his finger. 'Condensation, I should say...'

Hilda said quietly but cuttingly, 'The kitchen's a damned sight worse. We've found some prize specimens of fungus in there.' She pointed to the fireplace.

Menhennit stooped and examined the crumpled odiferous remains of the fluorescent toadstools. 'You found these in the kitchen?'

'Under the sink. I was going to keep them... they're rather splendid, botanically speaking, but not exactly welcome.'

Wrinkling his nose at the fungus, Menhennit straightened himself and said, 'I'll go and see.' He went into the kitchen.

'Terence,' said Hilda in a half whisper, 'Shall I tell him about... ?' She nodded towards the inner room.

Terence moaned softly to himself. 'Anything you like.

116

Please yourself... though I think it's best ignored.'

'Oh, but I feel we can't do that. It may be an important historical find.'

'Oh stuff the historical angle, Hilda! Leave the past alone, I say, and it won't do you any harm.'

'I can't agree with that. I have an awful premonition that if we don't do something...' She stopped, seeing the sneer writhing on his face as he silently mouthed the word 'Premonition...'

Menhennit came back frowning, holding something in his hand. 'Well, I must admit this baffles me. I've been handling the lettings for this place for five years at least, and everything's been perfectly all right till now.'

'No complaints about draughts, or lack of sanitation?' asked Terence.

'No sir. Nothing, that is, you could call complaints, in view of the very modest rent we charge. Most up-country people consider it a refreshing change, you know, to come down here and do without some of the luxuries of life... at least for a little while. But when it comes to this...' He held out a handful of greenish spongy substance. 'Moss,' he said in ponderously accusing tones. 'A good inch thick. In the laundry tub.'

It was true that Hilda was not one of those housewives who are always washing clothes. Innocently she said, 'How could you explain that, Mr. Menhennit?'

Menhennit had had certain qualities of the gentleman instilled into him by his Westcountry minor public school. It wasn't his place, he thought, to tell a lady – well, a woman, however artistic or bohemian – how often she ought to wash clothes. 'I must admit we have had it on the rainy side this past winter, and some of these old places do take a fair bit of drying out... Of course,' he said, noticing the paraffin heater and pouncing on it thankfully, 'these here things definitely don't help.' He tapped it balefully. 'Did you know,' he said to Terence, 'that these give out a gallon o' water vapour for every gallon of paraffin they burn? A good fire in the chimney is the only way to warm up these places, you take my word for it.' Challenging a seedy dyspeptic husband, who ought to be out doing some real work, was more in Menhennit's line of country, as he would have put it.

'Aha,' said Terence, warming to the confrontation. 'In other words' – he stood up and drew himself up to his full height of five feet, four and half inches – 'it's our fault, all this, eh?'

His peppery tone, and the implication that Hilda too was under attack, made Menhennit pause. 'I didn't exactly say that, sir. I'm merely considering all the points. Of course, a change in the weather could make a big difference.'

'It's quite clear,' said Terence, his shrill voice rising with a neurotic edge to it, 'that you suspect us of producing this... decay. You said yourself it never happened until we moved in.'

Menhennit considered. The senior partner of his firm liked a quiet life, and it was his job to keep clients contented, after all. He moderated his tone considerably. 'It could be a mere coincidence, no doubt. I didn't actually mean to imply...'

'Didn't you?' Terence almost shrieked. Something was growing in tension inside him, like a wire through his stomach and chest being drawn taut to breaking point. 'It was a pretty good insinuation, if you ask me. Well, let me tell you our conscience is clear; at least as clear as anyone else's.' He recognised that nobody could plead complete innocence from the evils of capitalism and economic exploitation; what happened to the smallholder who obviously once lived here? What right had he and Hilda to take his place? His voice rose further. 'We've nothing to hide, have we, Hilda? No dark and dirty secrets! We don't hold voodoo rites or perform black magic here, you know!'

'No, no, of course we don't,' Hilda said soothingly. Occasionally he did go slightly berserk, but she knew how to deal with him.

'Or even have sauna baths in the room, if that's what your're thinking!' raved Terence, his eyes staring maniacally.

'I didn't for one moment... ' began Menhennit, looking at this wild apparition with the shaking goatee beard.

Hilda took Terence's arm. 'Now sit down, dear, and get on

with your poems. Or maybe you ought to have some air – why not go for a walk while I discuss this with Mr. Menhennit?'

Terence sat down abruptly and stared out of the window.

'Please excuse his outburst,' Hilda said to the agent, 'he's been living on his nerves for a long time. It's the main reason we came away from London.'

'Oh, I quite understand, madam,' Menhennit said with clumsy gallantry. 'It can happen to all of us.'

Terence gave a bleak sharp laugh. 'Understand?' they heard him mutter to himself. 'Never in a million years...'

In an almost suicidal mood he folded his arms and contemplated the massing purplish-grey cloud outside, now threatening thunder over the peaked moors and bogs beyond.

Hilda drew Menhennit to the other side of the room. In a low voice she said, 'I feel I must mention that cupboard, Mr. Menhennit.'

'What cupboard, madam?'

'The big one in that room, with the heavy carved doors.'

'Ah yes?' said Menhennit. 'Is there anything the matter with it?'

'Not exactly. But it has... something in it.'

'Indeed?'

'Perhaps you'd like to go in and look?'

What was it, wondered Menhennit, that she didn't want to talk about? 'Very well, if you wish,' he said, and went to the door. Both Terence (though he maintained a detached attitude, with his back to the proceedings) and Hilda listened as the agent went in, crossed the room, and opened the cupboard. They heard him close the door, pause uncertainly, then come out rather more hastily that he had gone in. He returned with a blank dazed face, as if he had been sand-bagged.

'Well?' asked Hilda.

Menhennit said slowly, 'There's a skeleton in it. Gave me quite a turn, I don't mind admitting.'

'Exactly,' said Hilda with some satisfaction, speaking in

Terence's direction. 'You see now what we have to contend with.'

'I do indeed, ma'am. But I can't quite understand how it stands up.'

'*Stands?*' quavered Hilda.

'Absolutely upright, without any support. Did you wire it up? Very clever, if you did.'

'But, but,' said Hilda, almost crying, 'when we last looked... less than half an hour ago... it was only sitting!'

They stared at one another. Terence appeared frozen also. Then a loud distinct *clonk* came from within. 'My God,' Hilda said, 'there's that noise again. Did you hear? You must have.'

'I did hear something,' Menhennit said ponderously, striving for absolute calm. 'Probably a loose slate in the rafters. Wind's still rising.' Successive gusts were indeed crossing the moor and buffeting the cottage.

'It's getting worse all the time. And I must get to the bottom of it,' Hilda said desperately. ' I *know* there is an explanation, and I want it now. Mr. Menhennit: what is the exact history of this cottage?'

'History, ma'am?' repeated Menhennit. His eyes narrowed calculatingly, as if he was debating something with himself.

'Yes,' said Hilda firmly. 'It has a past. I know it. I feel it... here.' She was about to place her hands on her stomach, but with a glance at Terence's sullen back, put them on her breast instead. 'Something awful happened here. A long time ago. Am I right?'

'Well, now, as to that,' Menhennit said slowly, 'I couldn't say for sure, you understand.' He paused, then decided she should be trusted with what information he had. 'We had a lecture not so long ago at the Camelford Old Cornwall Society, by somebody pretty well up in the history of the Moor. Lady from over to Bodmin. And talking about this place, she reckoned that that old cupboard, as you call it, was a priest's hole in the old days. You know, the sort of place where the Catholics used to hide up their priests away from the Protestants? Now 'tis also very interesting, in my view' – his voice grew confidential and his large ruminant eyes stood out in his heavy face – 'that about two hundred years ago, a certain very attractive female party in this district was hanged for the murder of her husband; and the queer thing was they never found his body: only his hat and shoes.'

'Very pretty,' snapped Terence's voice. He had turned and was looking at them with something of his old cynical self. 'Just the kind of tale you people like to trot out to impress tourists, eh?'

'Yes,' said Menhennit. 'That's true enough. But I tell you this, sir: I've looked over that cupboard every time people have moved out of this cottage, checking over, you know... and I've never seen anything in it, let alone something like *that*.' He indicted the inner room with his thumb.

'Ah,' said Hilda in an awed voice. She sat down, pressing her hands together. 'I knew there was something. The pattern is becoming clearer. Don't you see? The bones, the damp, the mould – the fungus...'

'Mmmm... Frankly, though,' Menhennit said, 'I don't quite see what the mould's got to do with the skeleton.'

'It started to grow on the wall the day I found those bones lying there in the cupboard. It's been getting worse every day. Insistent, you might say.'

'Insistent?'

'I have the feeling,' said Hilda with a deep occult thrill in her voice, 'that those bones have been neglected for so long that... that they're crying out silently to us... to warn us against something... or maybe for help.'

'She'll be feeling sorry for them next,' said Terence.

Hilda knew he would scoff. But there was a presence on the other side of the door; one that would show itself soon, in fact any minute; and Terence, poor Terence, would have to come to terms with it despite himself. She only hoped it wouldn't be too much for him: she was afraid the balance of his neurotic mind would tip over into insanity. But she was helpless now to prevent that, if it should come. Something was definitely about to happen, and all she could do was wait.

'Well, in a way I sympathise, sir,' Menhennit was saying. 'I feel we ought to do something... give 'em a decent burial, somehow.'

'That's what I said.' Terence looked accusingly at Hilda. 'Why the hell didn't I throw them out and say nothing?'

'Oh no, it would surely be a crime to do anything like that,' Menhennit protested. 'I must inform the Society. They'll probably get the County Pathologist to look at them... 'Tis exciting, when you come to think of it. A real bit of Old Cornwall, eh?'

Terence turned and faced him, white with rage, his eyes aflame with the very madness Hilda feared. 'No! I absolutely forbid it. I'll destroy them, every spinal disc, kneebone and knuckle joint, if you call in anybody else. I will have peace and quiet here, at all costs.'

At which, by way of ominous warning, came the loudest *clonk* yet. It seemed to echo through their brains, hollow and spectral, mocking yet threatening; they stood transfixed. And Terence knew now he could do no more work, that he was being surely driven out by the remains, the presence, the occupant, whoever or whatever it was, in that room: an entity, a being who was coming now to claim the whole house.

'On the other hand,' he said abruptly changing his tone to one of rapid practicality, 'I may well emigrate. Go to Alaska, or the Sahara, or the Australian desert. Somewhere without people, where no one has ever wanted to live before... where there can be no past, only a future.' Were those his own words he heard his voice utter? He had no control over them, could only listen amazedly as they came out.

'I don't think that was a slate knocking,' said Menhennit, his face draining of colour.

Hilda said, with dreadful contemplation of some tremendous psychic force about to burst in upon them, 'It certainly wasn't. D'you think we ought to... see what is going on... in there?'

Menhennit turned yellow and seemed unable to reply. There was only one answer, thought Hilda. Terence, the unconverted, the unbeliever, must confront... it. 'Go in and see what it is, Terence, will you? We can't go on here... just waiting.'

Terence moved away from the inner door. 'Go and look

122

yourself, Hilda. I'm just not interested in your damned relics.' He had to convince himself that whatever it was didn't matter: that the future alone was now his concern. It seemed as good a defence as any in this situation. And Terence was no moral coward: his self-conceit and loyalty to his beliefs would not allow him to retreat. He hadn't stuck to his ultra-socialist line with all its contortions since the Nazi-Soviet pact of 1939 to be routed by a thing like this. He sat down at his typewriter and tapped out a few words, though he hardly knew what his fingers were doing. Before him on the paper appeared:

> Possibly some farm labourer jealous of his wife. Or a priest they forgot to let out and who starved to death. Perhaps even Fred Tresize with his boots full of clay waste.

Who cares? He thought. A new slate to write on, that's all I want. A glorious new destiny... He took a furtive glance behind him.

Hilda was actually taking Menhennit by the hand and going to the door. 'I think we must go in and see... don't you?' she was saying determinedly. Why, why? thought Terence. To hell with them! Bones, ligaments, dust, wind through dead men's ribs. Mere sound without the fury; empty husks and dried up kernels.

Three loud *clonks* like enormous supernatural drumbeats seemed to echo through the cottage. It was so dark now they could hardly see. Terence turned up the flame in the chimney of the oil lamp, but it made no difference. A spasm of sheet-lightning flashed over the moor towards Roughtor, followed by low distant thunder. Hilda and Menhennit retreated from the door, watching it breathlessly. With immense fortitude Terence went on typing.

> As I see it, the task before us now is to rid ourselves of the past, which has become a veritable millstone around our necks. As Henry Ford should have said, History is junk. What is this consciousness of the past, art and biology, archaeology and even psychology, but a load of rubbish cluttering up

123

our lives, preventing true self-exploration?

Behind him the handle of the door began to move, and squealed rustily: something was heard to scrabble at it from within, as if the instruments of contact could obtain no hold. Then slowly the brass handle moved, and Terence heard it. But the words went on appearing, feverishly, desperately now, with spelling mistakes and letters out of order, on the paper before him:

The fact is that the psat must be killed, must be exspunged,must leave us alone so that we cna look ahed without those stultifying ties or preconditionig, to build at last the true futture we all seak... A complety new world is surely the only hope fro us all now...'

And the door began to swing open with a loud slow groan. Hilda screamed: Menhennit rushed into the kitchen and out of the back door. A stronger flicker of lightning showed Hilda the fingers of a long skeletonal hand gripping the edge of the door.

Thick sweat stood out in icy globules on Terence's face, but nothing now would induce him to look behind. If necessary he would expire, protesting his new creed. He typed on:

A new world reserved exclusively for poeple like us who are no longer subject to irational impulses, metaphyscal omens, tribal myths, ! behavioral pattrens...'

Hilda saw what came through the door. That was all she could remember; immediately after she found herself running down the garden path amid the first fat drops of the storm. Menhennit's car was beginning to move off. She waved and screamed at him frantically, but he drove off into the pulsating darkness.

'Supperstitions' typed Terence's fingers as his eyes stared, mesmerised by the paper and fearful of what might next appear there. 'Ghost stroys or... SKELETONS IN THE CUP...'

Immediately behind him a rapid succession of those satanically vibrating *clonks* began: they seemed to throb throughout his being, racking and searing the nerves up the back of his head. The hair on his scalp bristled and lifted. His hands still went out to the keys, but he typed no more; he fell senseless over the typewriter, his hair beginning already to turn white.

Outside Hilda, now half-drenched by the increasing rain, ran up the lane amid the cosmic blinking of the lightning to find Janey Tresize.

IN KILLIGARREK WOOD

On a slowly fining Hallowe'en, after several days of blustering wind and rain when the landscape, parched following weeks of near-drought, was bursting with the suddenly revived fruits of late autumn, a young man and woman with a dog drove along a moorland road near St. Neot. He was fair and slightly built, with a thin dreamy face. His grey-blue eyes had a far-away look in them, the gaze of a hermit or philosopher. She was an attractive woman in her late thirties, confident, vivacious, determined. Her hair was cut short and styled in an attractive but businesslike fashion; her large jaw should have been a disadvantage to her but, perhaps because it spoke so well for her character, was a definite asset. She was driving; it was her car, a nearly-new Cavalier. The dog, a perky white-haired terrier, sat on the back seat, taking a keen interest in the countryside they were passing through.

'We're in luck with the weather, James, whatever else.'

'There'll still be boggy patches to get through, though,' he said. 'It rained again on the moors yesterday, I should say.'

They drew up where the road merged into a mere half-surfaced grassy track, which a few years previously farm vehicles had used. Two hundred yards up this lane stood several old buildings in poor repair, one with a collapsed slate roof. 'The farm house is abandoned now,' he said. 'There was no one there when I came before.'

'How long ago was that?'

'Two, maybe three years.'

'Did you come here alone?'

'Yes. Why?'

She gave him a warm, sympathetic glance. 'You don't seem to have many friends, that's all.'

'I have enough, but I don't presume on their company. Real friends seek one out.'

'Nobody seems to have time to do that nowadays. I have to

find mine, phone them, drop in on them, and maybe they secretly resent me. Maybe they pity me, I don't know.' The dog jumped out as she opened the door, and sniffed and worried his way up the track ahead. They took their anoraks, and she locked up the car. 'Though God knows who'll come hereabouts,' she said. They began to tramp briskly up the lane among profusions of blackberries, vibrant pink campion, rosehips, and blackthorns laden with sloes, many of them wrinkled and shrivelled.

'Why,' he said, brooding a little, 'should anyone pity you?'

'There are always a few happily married souls who think they ought to feel sorry for a divorced woman, and I've been married twice, remember. Of course,' she went on with brave, careless self-sufficiency, 'they're wasting their pity. I'm quite reconciled to my lot, and even happy on the whole. So long as I have one or two congenial friends or acquaintances to go on holiday with. I spend Christmas and other times with my parents, and see my children reasonably often, though they live in Leicester. And I have my teaching, which if you do properly, committedly, is very rewarding, you know.'

'I admire people who know what they want in life and get it. I wish I was like that.'

'Don't you know what you want?'

'Oh, I know a few things. I'd like eventually to settle down and marry, have children, I suppose. But just now I seem to have lost all purpose. A year or two ago I had all good intentions of being a writer of some kind. I wrote stories and poems, and even had a couple of things published. Then I began to study; I was going to create a new system of political philosophy. Now I'm learning Cornish and generally studying Celtic history. My father and I have continual rows over my drifting from one job to another, as he sees it. Clerking jobs, driving bread vans, delivering parcels. Can't say I blame him; it's so hard for his generation, brought up to get on, and go to Chapel every Sunday, to see that the old order has gone, and that we have to create a new one to replace it, or go under.'

127

She paused, and took his arm. Their faces were close together; she looked keenly into his eyes. Her own were brown, flecked with greenish and opalescent touches. Her gaze seemed to flow out to him, to submerge and wash over him. 'You know, you're really rather sweet – and somehow quite heroic,' she said softly.

'Heroic!' he repeated, and laughed a trifle nervously. 'No one ever called me that before.'

'Perhaps no one ever really understood you before.'

'Do you understand me?'

'I'm beginning to. Give me a little time, James. There's no hurry, is there?'

After all, they had only met properly the week before, though he had known her by name for some time. He had gone to a local dramatic society, offering to help with their latest production (an ambitious one, too; they were going to tackle *The Royal Hunt of the Sun*). He hadn't acted in anything since his school days, but vaguely felt that it might be an artistic outlet for his undirected nebulous desires. And Marika Carter was there as stage manager. As no one had thought to make this quiet newcomer welcome, she had decided that it was her duty to do so. Over a drink and a short chat in the bar after the meeting, at which he had been given the part of a soldier in Pisarro's expedition, they had taken to each other. She took him home with her for coffee, gently repelling the advances he had made, more out of a feeling that he would be expected to do so, than for any sexual attraction he felt; though he had recognised from the first greeting that she was a formidable and admirable woman. Twice married, twice divorced, though: it was intriguing and mystifying. Perhaps she had been just too much for both her husbands.

As yet he knew he mustn't question along these lines. Somewhere, he suspected, there was a fatal flaw in her, which had ruined all her relationships with men. If so, God help him if he became involved...

On the other hand, she might well be a discerning, fastidious person, still seeking from a man the respect and love that was so evidently due to her. He watched her striding a little ahead of him now, calling 'Gyp, Gyp,' to the dog, who was out of sight up the rising track, among hedges now dwindling and becoming sparse as they approached the real moor. He was aware that she was certainly more than a normal working woman: her actions, gestures, words, her tone of voice, all bespoke something beyond what he had so far encountered in the female sex.

He didn't rate himself as a great prize for any woman. He was far too sensitive of his own shortcomings, revealed during the few affairs (could they really warrant that description?) which he'd had so far. There had been a great garrulous overwhelming girl he'd gone to bed with in London once, on a weekend visit at her invitation. She'd enveloped him so completely that he'd felt like a lost soul wandering through the warm cloud of his own dissolution. In the morning she had looked at him with pity and dislike. There were others at various times and places, never entirely to his taste; some decidedly risky, once a young married woman. To put it quite realistically, he had never fully succeeded when it was expected of him, and he worried over this, especially at nights. Sometimes he wondered if, at the age of twenty-five, he was actually homosexual. Yet once when a middle-aged artist in his cups had made advances to him at a party, he'd shied away like a frightened filly. So he had reconciled himself to wait, to 'see what might betide' – the quotation (from Hardy, was it?) rising persistently from his subconscious.

They came out on to the open pristine moor, where cotton and bent grasses blew gently in ripples as the wind moved them, and heather and late-flowering Western furze took over from bushes and hedge flowers. To the north rose the humped skyline of Brown Willy and Roughtor, on the northeast, Brown Gelly; eastward were Sharptor and Caradon Hill with its forsaken engine houses. The sky arched, a pellucid inverted bell above them; at any moment he felt he would hear a distant tolling for mortal fortunes.

They passed by a group of low granite hut circles, memorials to the pre-Celtic Bronze age peoples who had actually farmed here on the damp, chill uplands. But, he reminded himself, the climate must have been warmer then, or they'd have all died from rheumatic fever or consumption.

The ancient Celts were a great source of fascination to him. More real and gripping than any novel, he bought and read eagerly any books he could find on their way of life; he had collected a considerable library of paper-backs and several hard-backs on the subject. He couldn't afford expensive tomes full of magnificent photos of Celtic gods, warriors or artifacts, and coloured reproductions of the Book of Kells; but little escaped his notice, and what he could not buy, he would borrow from the libraries, making copious notes from them. And he had made considerable progress already, after a mere couple of terms, in the language: Kernewek, or revived Cornish. One of his favourite pastimes, especially on dreamy, late summer evenings as darkness stole in from the east, was to sit in his room listening to the harps, flutes and binous of Stivell's music on records. At such times he was carried back, away into the longlost yet never forgotten world of Celtic heroism, legend and myth. Celts are supposed to be born with their heads looking back over their shoulders. Perhaps; but he knew it was that very quality of respect, indeed veneration, for the past which made Celtic tradition so persistent, so indelible and indestructible, despite all the horrors perpetrated against it by Roman and Germanic lusts for power. As he listened to such soul-soothing music, which stirred the very foundations of his being, he felt that despite the massacre at Anglesey, the defeat of Glendowr, the butchery at Culloden, and the iron suppression of Ireland, the true other-worldliness of the Celtic peoples would survive and triumph. For all that Flamank and An Gof had been hanged, drawn and quartered at Tyburn, that Cornish people had been taught for so long that they were English, that their own Bardic minstrelsy was lost and their language almost allowed to die, here was the prophetic harpist from Brittany speaking the language of music that echoed down the centuries, uniting them with their brothers and cousins in the vast rich heritage of the Celtic realm.

He walked slowly towards their goal, now overtaking Marika, who had suddenly stopped. Half a mile ahead, beyond the shrunken moorland stream which channelled its way through granite hollows, rose the hill on which grew Killigarreck Wood. Even from this distance it had a darkly secretive and forbidding aspect. The age-old oaks, elms and beeches stood closely together, a living wall, a palisade against the curious explorer. Not a leaf stirred in the quiet evening, yet a distinct low rushing and roaring emanated from the grove.

For a grove, a sacred Celtic enclosure, it undoubtedly was in James Trenance's eyes. Among all the groves in Cornwall, felled or thinned out and tamed, or turned to various insensitive agricultural purposes, this mighty moorland wood had been by-passed, left alone to brood and breed new generations of trees, whose ancestors had witnessed the whole rubric of Celtic rites and mysteries. For him, the fascination was such that he was impelled towards the place like a moth to the flame; though he was well enough aware of the evil reputation the place had in local minds. Marika was surveying the place with some dubiety. She shivered, zipped up her anorak, and put her hands in her pockets. 'I know I was sceptical before, but I feel there's something in there that forbids us, yet dares us to go in.'

This surprised yet gratified him. She possessed a psychic, perhaps historically sympathetic dimension, he thought. He put his arm protectingly around her. 'I know there are all sorts of ignorant superstitions about the place,' he said. 'Tales of people being murdered there, and found dead with their hair turned white. But really, there's nothing to fear, I promise you.'

'Well, you have actually been in there, haven't you?' She sought reassurance from him, her eyes searching his.

'Yes, I went inside all right.'

'What's it like in there?'

'Mysterious. Eerie. But certainly compelling.'

'What time of day was it?'

'Early afternoon, I think. But it's so dark in there, that even at that time it was hard to see anything. Come on...'

He moved forward, taking her arm. She followed, slowly, without fear now, but thoughtfully. The dog Gyp, twenty yards ahead of them, had been nosing happily along, following various trails and scents; now he stopped, his tail and ears cocked, and looked back.

'He can sense something,' Marika said. 'It's all right, Gyp. Come on, boy. Come with us.'

The three moved forward down the track to the stream, and over the large boulders which acted as stepping stones. As they reached the other side the dog whined and pawed the ground. He looked up imploringly at his mistress' face as if pleading to go back.

'What's up, Gyp?' James said gently. 'Nothing to be frightened of, old chap.'

'Come on then,' said Marika. She took James by the arm, and together they climbed the last four hundred yards to the first oaks of the grove.

'The thing to remember,' James said now, ' is that for the ancient Celts, the groves were places of worship and powerful magic.' He had wondered whether Marika would even listen to his theories; now she was a captive audience. 'I believe you can pick them out by names on maps up and down Cornwall. Kelly means grove. It means so little to us today, but to them... these were places where the most important religious rites were held. Where Gods were worshipped.'

'Where they performed human sacrifices?'

'No doubt. They were supposed to propitiate their Gods with the lives of their captured enemies. Caesar tried to root out the Druids and the groves, cut them down wherever he could. But there's so much more to Celtic religion than mere sacrifice. I wish I knew which of the Gods or Goddesses were worshipped here.'

What he stopped short of telling her was that at Samhain, or Hallowe'en, when the Celtic year ended and began, the gods were said to appear and walk among men.

They now paused only a few yards from the first trees, peering into the apparently impenetrable interior. Marika said, 'I'm a pagan, through and through; I admit it. And this

132

terrifies me, yet compels me... You're right, there's something almost irresistible in there, drawing us in to prove something...'

She started forward, breathless and wide-eyed, and looked at him. Then she laughed loudly, almost drunkenly, and plunged on, dragging him in with her. A moment later they were out of the brilliant evening sunshine and in the dense gloom of the wood.

The first thing they became aware of was the sound of rushing water, eddying and swirling around them. It seemed to come from all sides, retreating, then deluging them. It was more than water noises however; it seemed to carry overtones of dirge-like music, like the wind blowing through ancient harps.

As their eyes became slowly adjusted to the darkness, they saw mighty contorted limbs of trees, gnarled and swollen branches, huge boles with deeply etched wrinkles and scorings that seemed to be part of an omnipresent ageless design; as if between them all they summed up to a maze of intricate Celtic designs. But in the deep shadows these very trunks and branches seemed to advance and retreat, to writhe and coil like immense serpents, the tails of which flowered and branched into twigs and leaves, whose roots and trunks grew faces and features that momentarily assumed the aspect of known and unexpected things. Each serpent seemed to have a ram's head, with convoluted inspiralled horns, until they looked at it closely and it became, maddeningly, a mere tree again. Further ahead, a sinuous form assumed a human bodily shape, but with the antlered head of a stag: the trunk glistened and turned, the multifoliate horns swayed and lifted.

On their left, the great stump of a former oak reared up with bullish aspect and roared at them; birds with plumed heads swooped upon him, and he plunged as they alighted on his back. Only there were no birds in here at all. Marika realised this, looking about her: the leaves above joined and interweaved into a dense canopy which physically forbade them to enter.

The water noises grew in volume as they moved forward,

both possessed by the all-powerful atmosphere. They walked between lush ferns and creepers, the ground becoming soft underfoot, until they saw the dark glimmering of water. A fast stream, tumbling down over rocks smoothed by centuries, plunged into a lake at the further end, and the cascading water rang about them like chimes of bells.

Across the lake the tendrils of maidenhair fern moved silently, as if a breeze or person moved through them; yet no breath of air was to be felt. A great shimmering presence gathered beneath them in the waters, luminous but shapeless. They stood dazzled by it, and the water music seemed to rise and echo to a climax as it swam up towards them; until, looking up, James descried, through a small patch where the branches thinned, the clear, bright disc of the moon.

'Nemetona, moon goddess,' he breathed, and knelt. Marika did the same, without question, instinctively. 'Show us your mysteries. Admit us to your rites,' he intoned. '*Dysqua dhyn-ny dha nerth, Dewes vur.*'

These words came into his mind without thought or effort; some of them he had never learnt.

Marika moaned softly, regarding him with the gaze of a devotee. He had become the druid, priest of the grove: he was initiated, could invoke all the gods of the Celtic pantheon; she was his acolyte, his temple prostitute, his slave. Looking at her, he saw it all in her eyes. But greater desires than that of a man for a woman possessed him.

Nemetona rose higher as they stared at each other, transfixed. Then he took her softly by the hand and bade her rise. Slowly they undressed, without thought, possessed by a joint unspoken intention they could not disobey, and together they entered the lake. The dark water closed around their naked flesh with a chill yet inviting sensation, a sober revivifying touch. Once in the pool they laughed, clasped each other and kissed in innocent, almost bodiless joy.

'Sing out for the spirit of the hills,' he shouted, 'sing for the purifying gift of water, and the life force in rocks and streams. *Canen gans oll agan gallos.*' And Marika, who had a

134

fine soprano voice, sang a wordless chant, echoing, soaring among the great branches, weaving a glistening web of song between the massive, immemorial trees. He stood entranced, worshipping her now, his feet embedded in the shingle bed of the lake. They came out, cold but glowing almost phosphorescently, lit from within by their obsessions and beliefs.

Without more ado he stood in an attitude of invocation, his arms outstretched and his head uplifted. '*Deugh, deugh, Tarannos, Cernunnos, Esos, Rosmerta ha Nantoseulta...*' The words issued from his mouth in a rich, thundering bass, so far removed from his own high soft tenor as to cause her to shudder, believing him possessed by demonic supernatural powers. '*Deugh dhyn-ny, deugh an Vatres, Lugh Mur ha'n Dagda ynweth, deugh oll dhyn-ny.*'

His body stiffened, shook with a spasm of muscular ague, and he felt the blood beating up through his chest, neck and temples. She cried out and, fainting, fell across him. Together in an insensate embrace they lay there. Somewhere in the outskirts of the wood an owl crooned softly, almost a growl. And a great surge of turning leaves swept through the wood, though outside the air was as still as a morgue.

☆☆☆

Snakes writhe around the trees, and reach up to vanish and reappear in the upper branches. Trunks quake and give off fire-glow, though without flames. The carved heads of gods look on, each an immense trunk shaped to the form of a deity; Lugh and Dis, Nemetona, Bran, Tarannis and Esos.

A fire flickers somewhere, amid a pall of smoke. The sound of scores, perhaps a hundred people breathing; then breathless, holding their breaths. A skin, drawn tight over a hoop, drummed on lightly by fingers: another joining it; a third, a fourth, until all around the sacred grove the light tapping rises in volume and the invocation is everywhere, beating up from the ground, throbbing into the blood, pulsing through every leaf and branch.

The white-robed Druids approach the fire, one holding a sheaf of wheat saved from the previous year's harvest, the

135

second bearing flowers in an intricately woven garland, the third wine and cheeses. The offerings are cast on the fire, each with a prayer. The gifts burn richly, giving off fumes like incense; the aroma reaches the waiting Celts, who begin to chant:

'*Gans tan gor uskys sacryfys;*
'*Dh'agan dewow ny a'n-re.*'

And the Archdruid, and old man, is suddenly glorified in the fire-light: his arms raised, the robes draping him shot with flame and invested with red and gold glories, his flowing white locks shining, he cries:

'*Deugh dh'agas tuatha, dewow vur ha Keltek. Kemer agan sacryfys, ny-'gas-pys.*' And the crowded figures hush, sinking to their knees, as from the shadows behind them the first dreaded figures emerge: a triad of goddesses, the Matres, with long flowing hair down over their ample bodies and full swaying breasts. The first holds a lusty infant on her hip, the second a great cornucopia full of grain, and the third a basket of luscious, rosy fruits. They pause to smell the burning corn and spicy wine, smiling and turning to the worshippers in benediction, before fading back into the swirling fumes and darkness.

The druids now bring forward a colt; two of them hold it, hobbled by a golden plaited rope, while the high priest cuts its throat with a golden-hilted knife. The chanting of the worshippers grows in volume. The blood pours out, the animal sinks to its knees, its head jerking in convulsions. Cast into the fire, the sudden smell of its burning flesh and hair assault the nostrils of those watching. As the animal's struggles cease and the life force ebbs from its already burning carcass, another goddess emanates from the gloom, seated on a white mare, and followed by a foal. The Archdruid cries, '*Epona, Epona, ro dhyn-ny bennath, ha bennath dh'agan hendasow marow.*'

This is a haughty deity, her glance imperious and condescending. Her white steed paws the ground, as if seeking to ride the waves of emotion she raises in them all. The two worshippers apart from the rest (not James and

Marika now, but two persons of the time, two previous incarnations or alter-egos) recoil, cover their eyes and cry out with the others to the protectress of the living and the dead:
'*Epona, Epona, gwyth adhyworthyn-ny drok oll.*'
The colt's carcass is consumed, the fire stoked higher with branches, bracken leaves and turves. The flames throw out figures of light around the grove, reaching into the avenues of darkness and revealing severed heads on pillars of the temple, some of them gory with bloodstains; also the statues of human warriors with shields and spears, and a huge stone eagle. Over the temple a basketwork roof rises, from which hang death-masks of kings and heroes. Epona, her mount and foal have vanished.

Now a great white bull is led forward, docile enough at first; then he bellows as he is brought nearer the fire, well suspecting his fate. He is roped by each of his legs. His long horns thrash the air, and his powerful neck and head strain away, the crimson eyes now terrified. Strong men come forward to assist the Druids; finally he is brought to the fire, and his throat is cut with a great bronze knife. With a choked spasm, he sinks to his knees, the life blood gushing out in a pool that soon mingles with the waters of the lake.

The Archdruid now invokes the name of Nemetona, Moon Goddess, Goddess of war, the Fury who brings fate and retribution to those who violate ancient Celtic laws. She descends in a cloud of white frost, and a shiver runs through the worshippers; the white bull quivers and subsides into the stillness as, standing with one foot on its head, she raises her arms, a carved sword in one hand and silver shield like a round moon in the other. The worshippers sink down, not on their knees now, but their bellies, faces to the ground. The two apart follow suit. '*Nemetona, Nemetona, dewes vur agan casow, gwyth adhyworthyn an jawl, ha gul droklam war agan yskerens,*' the voices moan and murmur, none daring to meet the implacable, ice-cold glance of the deity. She signs a blessing upon them, then suddenly is gone, faded, immaterialised into a white vapour that lingers to die out among the trunks and branches of the glade. The fire, which has sunk back to mere smouldering embers at her coming,

137

now revives and flames again as the Druids heap turves and tinder on it.

Lugh is next: the Shining One, the Celtic Mercury, with his spear which thirsts for blood, and it is a fine hunting hound they sacrifice to him; master of the arts, father of Cu Chulainn, the great hero, Lugh blesses them opulently, scattering wisdom through the air, so that for a moment they are full of knowledge, dreamers of old dreams and visionaries of time to come.

Now comes the Dagda, Father of All, Lord of Perfect Knowledge, whose harp controls the seasons; his sacrifice is a comely maiden, who proudly steps forwards to offer herself. But no death scene here, for the Great Good God, a vaster Pan, rising hugely from the earth itself before the flames, takes her to him. His shaggy beard covers his body to his belly; his shambling gait belies his immense fecundity which has fathered seventy children on Morrigan and Boann. The ravished maiden cries out in ecstasy and falls naked and insensate to the ground, almost into the flames. The people are hushed and stilled again; the Dagda surveys them all tenderly and takes her up, reviving her with a single breath into her nostrils. He returns her to her people, and sinks back into the earth, blessing his worshippers with rich, coarse laughter.

After the Dagda is Cernunnos. The springs of desire released by the Great Father are now brought to rushing torrents by the Lord of Beasts and Fertility, with his spreading stag horns and fishtail, holding his serpent with a ram's head. A sudden tremendous atmosphere of communal lust and bodily desire possess the assembly as he appears, naked apart from the golden torque which swings from his neck. Woman prostrate themselves, crying out to be his sacrifice; but the Druids bring out a mighty ram, his wool plaited and combed into intricate patterns and Celtic knots, his involuted horns burnished like brass; they bring him to a waiting ewe. As the proud male animal mounts his mate, all shout, '*Gwra kerensa, gwra sawena, Cernunnos agan Dew!*'

And Cernunnos passes among them as men couple with

138

women, inspired by his darkly glowing erotic presence. The two watching slowly turn to embrace each other, locking themselves in the profound passion of a love which is older, more instinctive, more irresistible than any they have ever known. They give themselves utterly to each other, to forces greater than themselves; they are possessed by their own urges, magnified and exalted in the immemorial rhythm of the earth, renewing itself for as long as it bears life.

Darkness. The sound of water, drooling and singing among stones. A vast stillness: each fern leaf, every stamen and pistil in the cavern of foliage over the grove is silent, unwavering, at rest. The Gods have departed and the very earth itself sleeps in a holy aftermath, a deep miasma, a profound unbreakable coma. Samhain has come and gone for another year.

The two watchers, still locked together, become gradually aware. They see nothing in the impenetrable darkness, but the smell of burnt offerings remains in their nostrils. Passion spent, slowly they draw apart, then embrace again in a new estimation of themselves as man and woman, lover and beloved. They touch each other, they worship anew, this time with the sacred, almost virginal caresses of strangers. Without words they know each other, and are sure.

Leaving the grove, still unspeaking, they walked hand in hand down the slope towards the stream in the gathering dusk. The dog Gyp whined from a nearby thicket and rushed up to them, full of delirious greeting. They smiled at each other and went, arms round one another, across the stream and down to the car. Over the far downs the risen moon shone like an announcement of cosmic good news. But they alone, it seemed to them, shared the knowledge of its true significance.

Once in the car, they broke into an animated conversation that seemed uncontrollable; as if now released from a dark trance, they sought refuge and consolation in the small chat of modern civilisation. But after a while, as they proceeded out to the main roads of present-day Cornwall, James said, 'Marika, do you think this experience of ours – in the grove – can ever be repeated?'

She thought a moment before replying, 'Perhaps. But does it matter if it isn't? Surely once is enough?'

'I suppose so. I feel transfigured – a new man – a real man. At last.'

'You'll always be that for me. The first real man I've ever known, ever truly loved.'

'Are you sure?'

She stopped the car and kissed him, her eyes brimming with emotion. 'We'll worship in our own way, my Druid, my high priest, my lover-hero, my fertility god, my...'

He stopped her lips with his fingers, laughing softly, a gleam of foreknowledge in his eyes.

On the horizon, Nemetona, the moon, rode up into a clear heaven.

THE REVENANT OF PRIORY HOUSE

Lodenek: a summer afternoon in the 1980s. The inner harbour crowded with sailing craft, speedboats and pleasure cruisers loading with passengers; scores of visitors in holiday attire perambulating across the quays, eating ice-cream or fish-and-chips; herring gulls silently begging from those resting on public seats, pouncing on scraps and squabbling with each other; men and boys in lurid shirts patiently watching fishing lines strung out from the piers. Across the river beyond the outer jetties, the sand dunes and pine groves of the northern shore of the estuary.

Leaning on the parapet of the ancient arched porch of her home, reached by a flight of slate steps, Matilda viewed the passing concourse below her with distinct distaste. She appeared a wild figure, with haunted grey eyes, her white hair standing out in a shock; she muttered incessantly to herself, sometimes gabbling out her perpetual monologue loudly enough for the passers-by to hear, pause, and laugh at what they discerned. Matilda didn't understand this modern world; it fascinated and puzzled her. But her life was almost over, and she lived now mainly in the past, among her memories.

Who am I? She would often ask herself; and because there was no one else to answer, she would reply: I am myself, yet not myself. I live in this old house, the oldest in Lodenek, and people look at me as if I'm a ghost. Perhaps I am more ghost than person, a stranger in this town I've known so well since the nineteen-thirties. Yes, I'm a revenant, dead to everyone but myself.

She watched young couples walking hand in hand, viewed men without shirts, blandly showing red chests and hairy bellies, women in suntops and bikinis, and bickering children in shorts and sandals. She shuddered at the gross aromas of parading humanity, body sweat and suntan lotion mingled with the stale smell of fried fat. There was a time, she told them all in her slightly cracked, piercing voice, when fish-and-chips was a meal to overjoy the stomach, not a mere greasy snack served up in plastic trays to litter up the quayside and harbour.

They didn't sympathise. 'Look at the old dame up there,' called one, in a Brummagem accent.

'Ah, she's crazy, chuntering away to herself all day...'

'Yeah, silly old bat.' – A really Cockney voice, that one.

'Come away, you children, don't stare.' – A slightly genteel parent trying to impose a dying code of manners on her offspring.

Of course you all think me mad, don't you? Matilda told them. But who's mad, who's sane in this crazy world of yours? You'll find out, you ignorant yahoos, when I throw a bucket of water down on you. Yes, I've done it more than once, never you fear. That young fisherman found out the other day. Painting his boat on a Sunday morning with his transistor going full blast. Horrible screaming rock music. Couldn't even hear me shouting at him. So I a took a nice half-rotten apple I was going to give to the gulls, and threw it; nice shot, got him just behind the ear. So surprised he dropped his paintbrush in the mud.

She cackled loudly, a rasping crazy sound, causing more upward glances, nudges and grins.

Serves him right, desecrating the Sabbath. I don't know what's happening to our dear old town... Every year its gets worse, the noise and nuisance, the filth and the smells...

She looked out over the harbour, at the green tide swinging the boats at their moorings, hardly seeing them or the pleasure craft full of trippers. The sun, now lowering towards five o'clock, caused the slate roofs of the tall waterfront buildings, most of them former grain stores and warehouses, to gleam with white heat. She stared at them with glazed eyes.

I'm a ghost, all right. Matilda, you're a ghost, don't you know that? A crazy old revenant, living in the oldest, the most haunted house in all Lodenek. Oh yes, I know all the ghosts here, every shade and spirit. There's that pale silly servant girl, the one who's supposed to have hanged herself in the room up above. Got herself pregnant, no doubt. And

142

that funny spaniel-like dog, with white pearly staring eyes, that runs down the back stairs so silently. And of course the Reeve, as I call him, drifting about in his grey habit. Who was he? Wish he'd speak to me. Perhaps he ran the house in the days of the monastery. About 1520 or so, nearly five hundred years ago. He'd probably have been in charge of the place when it was the port Toll House, collecting tithes and fish dues and landing charges. Yes. Priory House, we call it now. Had its own chapel, right alongside here on the quay. Pulled down when Henry or Elizabeth sold off whatever they could get their royal thieving hands on...

She stared up at the medieval moulding and the arch over the porch, carved in grey-green elvan from the Cataclewse quarries four miles west. Beyond were two sightless crudely sculpted heads in the same stone, one a lion's, the other an antelope's, set in niches in the crumbling slate wall.

I'll wager those carvings came from the old chapel. That opening in the wall beside the cellar door: supposed to be a leper's window, through which they fed the poor devils chained up inside. Then later this was the Guildhall of the Lodenek merchants. They built the first stone jetty here about 1580. Flourishing little port, trading with Ireland... Sir Walter Raleigh here, Lord Lieutenant of Cornwall, raising troops and fitting out an expedition to land in Cork, to conquer those rabid Gaels for his Queen... And how did she reward him?

The voices of people below, the blatant jangle of a pocket radio, and the sudden magnified wasp-voice of a motor-scooter, cut across her thoughts; she shuddered inwardly, but went on remembering.

I see it all, the whole panorama of history leading up to this. Charles II, then Prince, supposed to have escaped from Devereaux House through a tunnel leading down to below this house; Roundheads in pursuit. Doubt if an under-ground passage that long could be made. There is a sort of deep alcove in the cellar, though, all blocked up with rubble... Maybe, if excavated... Timber and amber imported from Norway in the eighteenth century. Then in the nineteenth, emigrants sailing out to Canada, grain brought back. Ankers of brandy smuggled in from Brittany. Lifeboat disasters, two lost in one night in 1900. Those people down there have no idea of what went on. Ignorant pitiful fools! But what's the use of such knowledge, hoarded up by a scatty old hermit like me, marooned here amid a tide of phillistinism, materialism, cacophony and crass pleasure? I could write books, give lectures, teach 'em all about the past. And I used to, of course: I'd almost forgotten my talks to the W.I., The Methodist Sisterhood, the Old Cornwall Society... so many years ago. Nineteen-fifties. Lodenek appreciated, respected me then. What have I come to now?

She thought of her youth, of the Girton education which she'd brandished like a flaming torch. Young and full of enthusiasm, she had spoken out and lived for her ideals. Who had benefited? A good question. Well, the Marshall children, at least, she supposed...

Her mind went back to those summers before the war, in the mid or late nineteen-thirties, when as governess to Henry Marshall's children she used to accompany the family down to Cornwall in the great Lagonda, to stay here at Priory House. Henry, then a spruce young businessman (he came from the family which owned fifty high-class clothing stores across the country) would be up in front with the chauffeur. On the wide back seat would be Matilda herself with the first Mrs Marshall and the small children; George, seven or eight, and Clarissa, a couple of years older. Either Edward or Sophie, the oldest, would sit up in front with their father, or behind in the open dickey-seat, breeze-blown and thinking themselves lords of all creation.

But in Cornwall Matilda was their guardian, their mentor, their constant referee on the glorious beaches, the river foreshore and the cliffs.

We collected semi-precious stones, agate and crystal, topaz and amethyst; I still have my collection, gathering dust on the shelves... In those days we seemed to have the whole coast to ourselves. The day we found a starfish with only three arms. I had to explain, it would soon grow two more. The fishermen used to tear them up when they found them, because they eat mussels and whelks, but that only made more starfish in time.

Yes, she could feel the warmth of those far-off summers even now, bringing more memories: warmth on their backs and sun-hatted heads as they found snake-locks anemones far out at low spring tide in Trevone Bay; as they watched oystercatchers probing the weed-covered rocks for sea-lice, or prizing limpets off the smooth slatey surfaces; as they spotted fulmars gliding effortlessly along the cliffs at Tregudda: they had just begun to nest along this coast then...

I organised expeditions to various bays, and boat trips; sometimes we went fishing for mackerel. Edward was always horribly sea-sick, poor boy... But from the first I was in charge. Frances abdicated all power and responsibility to me.

Frances, Henry's first wife, had been a wilting flower, ailing since she 'came out' in 1922. She was anaemic, forever lying down with headaches and palpitations. The strain of bearing four children couldn't have helped.

So Henry would naturally fall back on me to take her place at the play or the opera. Eventually, after she died, I became his hostess at parties. Always a great observer of the proprieties in his home was Henry, but I knew his feelings for me long before he spoke of them. Never so much as touched me, except when we danced. Never approached my room. No surreptitious kisses. But he knew exactly what he wanted, and within a month of Frances' death we were unofficially engaged.

Matilda looked down at the engagement ring she wore next to her wedding one, a proud diamond set in a circle of tiny sapphires which glistened and flashed with minute points of flame.

He bought me this, oh, three months I suppose afterwards, when we all threw off our mourning. A day of great joy, and great distress, when he told them. The children were divided about me. Clarissa especially; she'd been very fond of Frances. And I'd been so sure of them all, a mother to them as well as a firm but kind governess.

She sighed. The sun swung down behind the trees above the town, and shadows of buildings and boats were lengthening across the quays.

Time I had some tea. A saffron bun, yes, and perhaps some of that Stilton before it walks out of the cupboard...

In her shabby carpet slippers, one split down the heel, she shuffled into the one room in which she lived: full of old newspapers and magazines, her books scattered across shelves and table and in piles on the floor, her ancient HMV gramophone, her cherished shells and stones on the mantelpiece. Into the kitchen she went, struck a match and lit the ancient gas stove, and put the heavy iron kettle on it. The kettle had been bought for the Cornish kitchen range she never used now; she'd never got around to buying a lighter, more efficient utensil.

Still, her thoughts meandered as she rinsed out her teapot and prepared her simple meal, Edward accepted her. The eldest boy, about fourteen at the time. Never forgets to send me a Christmas card; Sophie sends too, now and again. My birthday, though, forgotten by them all. Haven't had a birthday card from anybody for ages. Forget the date myself most years. Only to be expected: they've all got their own families now. I'll never see any of them again. Why should they be interested in a pensioned-off old ghost, safely out of the way in a little fishing port?

Yet once she'd had high expectations of her proxy family, envisaging visits from them and their children, and she'd hoped to go up to stay with them in town. Why shouldn't it have been like that?

Wasn't I good enough to them? Good enough for them? I come from as good a family; better, no doubt, if you want to be snobbish. Their chain stores, high-class merchandise, yes; but it still only makes them bourgeois middle-class shop-keepers. I wasn't too proud, too aristocratic, to take service with the Marshals – *noblesse oblige*, in a way. Dear father couldn't keep me at home, but after all we were related to the Sackvilles. Did I really deserve this?

Henry Marshall had died, leaving her Priory House in trust for her life, and five thousand pounds invested in Gilt Edged stock to provide for its upkeep; and that didn't go far these days. So the building was slowly deteriorating, with a leaking roof, peeling wall paper, and rising damp.

Some rooms I simply daren't go in for fear of what I might find. Not my problem so long as I have a room or two to live in, and keep dry. If they want the house passed on to them in good condition they should come down and see it – and me. What would Henry think now? Ah, Henry... You did love me, indeed I know you did.

The kettle boiled. She made the tea strong, as she liked it, and drank it with sugar but no milk.

With me all his latent boyish passion, so long suppressed by boarding school – Marlborough it was, yes – and his army service (Major in the Hampshire Rifles) and all those weighty business matters, board meetings and so on... with me his feelings sprouted, flourished in our bedroom like the great bay tree. We knew what love was in the early days of our marriage...

She bit into the yellow bun and found it dry and stale. It had been bought almost a week before.

Put some butter on it. I'd toast it if I could be bothered.

She got the butter from the cool cupboard (she possessed no refrigerator), hoping it hadn't gone rancid.

Seems all right, she thought, masticating slowly. None of those fancy margarines or spreads for me. Just a trick to exploit people who want to keep their weight down. All rubbish, if you ask me.

She sipped her tea, thinking, but who's asking? Nobody. Wonder what day it is. Tuesday, Wednesday? I forget so often; only the church bells on Sunday bring me back to the awareness of time. Strange thing, time. What's it composed of? Time ebbs and flows like the tide. It besieges me here like the sea round a rock. What have I to do with time, stranded here on a far shore, awaiting death? That's all I'm doing, really. Face it, Matilda, you're only waiting for the end; and it may come soon. Sometimes I think I'm actually timeless; I've outlived my use to anyone, including myself. And yet I had my times, for all that, and wonderful and precious they were. Nobody can take them away from me now; I relive them over and over again, week in, week out. That's what keeps me going.

She remembered now, with immediate and startling actuality, as if he'd come suddenly into the room, Henry's voice, soft with longing, his words caressing her in the night. 'Let me see you in the moonlight,' his quiet, fastidious voice came back to her over the years. 'Such a firm young figure you have, my dear, so supple and straight. Take your nightdress off, Matilda, let me see the moonlight play on your white body...'

And she had taken off her satin nightdress with its flower-embroidered bosom, one of his wedding presents to her; and sat still as a statue on the bed, breathing quietly, her breasts rising and falling as she stared at him with a faint smile. He leaned forward and kissed her shoulder, her bosom, her belly, her thighs. 'What a sight you are,' he whispered. 'As lovely as the Venus de Milo... with her arms restored...'

She recalled their honeymoon, also here at Priory House, with only a daily woman to do for them. They had gone for long cliff walks, to Hawker's Cove and Stepper point, around to Butterhole and Seal Hole and Gunver Head, to the booming chasm of Tregudda Gorge, and on to Marble Cliffs and Porthmissen Bay. And one day he had made love to her, in an old overgrown cliff quarry high above the seething, crashing waves, as oystercatchers piped below on the rocks and the herring gulls carped, sailing above them.

I brought out the latent savage in him. Very few people walked the cliffs for pleasure in those days. But there might have been boys out there after gulls' nests, a coastguard on his way to the lookout, or a fisherman going out for bass; neither of us would have cared, so much we were in love and wanting each other. I remember so vividly the day I dared him to come swimming, and we ran naked into the breakers at Harlyn... April it was; into the icy shock we plunged and my God it was cold and he shook and turned blue, but insisted on keeping up with me as I swam out and out; then I took pity on him and came in, just in time I think or he'd have collapsed... I think it was too much for him. He was never quite the same afterwards.

They had had only three years together before he suffered a heart attack at fifty-two. Had she really killed him, she still wondered, agonising over it – a mere guileless girl of twenty-six, unused to men? Had she caused him to act so young, when he was greying into middle age, and getting out of condition?

The young have no conception of age – how should they? Stiff joints and slowing heart and breath, the aching in the bones and failing memory... Ah, memory, memory... failing or not, I still have my memories. They say as you get older you remember your youth in more vivid detail. Sometimes I seem to be all memory, a shade living in the past, without wireless or television or newspapers to remind me of the terrible world they all live in, out there.

She finished her bun, washing the last mouthful down with tepid tea. She rinsed out her cup, saucer and plate under the cold tap (there was no hot water system in the house, she depended on the kettle for washing up, and never had a bath nowadays since the old gas geyser in the bathroom didn't work); and dragged back in her worn-out slippers to the living room.

Come and go so fitfully though they may, what would I be without these memories? A husk, an empty shell, a piece of stranded flotsam with no reason to go on.

She went over to the bookcase and fingered with love and nostalgia the well-worn volumes on its shelves. Here were her favourite books, read scores of times; they too were now really relics of the past, of her youth, her education. *Northanger Abbey, The Forsyte Saga*, poems of Keats, Shelley, Wordsworth, *Paradise Lost, Peter Abelard* by Helen Waddell, *Sons and Lovers, Middlemarch, The Waste Land, The Four Quartets*. And Donne, which she now picked up, turning the pages.

Dear lively, loving John Donne. My small select library; no need for anything else. Henry never understood that sort of thing. Not a reader. Too commercially minded. But kind and considerate; he took immense pride in me. Used to read to him sometimes, out of Wordsworth or George Eliot, sometimes darling Jane. He said he loved the sound of my voice, like a river running on, singing a lullaby. Then as if to prove it he'd fall asleep...

149

But we did have our moments, crammed as they were into those three years or so. He was a good dancer, a passionate dancer. From the first, I found, he'd seize every occasion to dance with me. Oh those Charlestons and foxtrots, sambas and rhumbas. And the bands, Joe Loss and Henry Hall and Victor Sylvester... Let's have a little taste of it all now.

She went to the old HMV and turned the handle to wind it up, examining it lovingly, the polished rosewood cabinet with small doors at the front, covering the speaker; and selected a record from the pile of shellac 78-speed discs lying on the bottom shelf of the bookcase. She put it on; there was the soft hiss of the wooden needle as the slow rhythms of saxophone, drums and strings enveloped her. Holding her arms across her bosom she swayed dreamily in time with it, staring at the revolving black disc.

All tape recorders and long playing records now. Wouldn't be bothered with 'em if they gave 'em to me. Tried steel needles, but they make too much surface noise.

Wood ones were more mellow, but of course you had to sharpen them so often. She had only three left; when they were worn down perhaps she herself would be worn out. The music swooned and swerved about her, bringing back those heady days of the thirties – *entre deux guerres*, as T.S. Eliot called them – the uncertain emergence from the years of the Depression, the wilful refusal to recognise danger growing in Europe...

Ah, Henry, Henry... I remember so well our times together... The Chelsea Arts Ball, Ascot Week, the Company outings... and those parties our business friends gave for their children's twenty-firsts or Coming Out... We danced on the Queen Mary when we went to New York – when was it, 'Forty Seven or Eight I suppose... drinking Bollinger, your favourite. A bit sharp for me, I always preferred gin and It.

She gazed fondly now at the faded wedding photograph of herself and Henry on the mantelpiece: she in a chic suit with hat and veil, holding a bouquet of narcissi, lilies and tulips: he in a lounge suit. A quiet wedding at Caxton Hall, which had upset most of Henry's orthodox Jewish family; Matilda, an agnostic as most Vicar's daughters were then,

150

only compounded the sin. But several of his more broad-minded relatives came, and his children of course; though one or two of them sulked and wouldn't speak to their new stepmother. But it was all lively enough at the reception at the Park Lane Hotel. George, then fifteen, got quite drunk, and Sophia, twenty-two, was lusted after by several of Henry's business friends who pawed her and breathed cigar and after-shave fumes all over her...

We danced most of the evening, Henry and I, until about midnight; then went to bed at the hotel. He was too tired to make love then, though I was ready enough; but in the morning, with the sun peering in through the heavy curtains (I quoted Donne at him – 'Busy old fool, unruly sun, Why dost thou thus Through windows and through curtains call on us?')... then... I became a married woman indeed. O Henry, dear Henry; so little time together... Perhaps I wanted too much from you. Did I wear you out? Did you have any regrets? The night of your attack...

How could she ever forget that night? They had been to the Lord Mayor's Dinner and heard the Prime Minister speak: Sir Winston Churchill himself. November 1951. Coming home in the cab they had never been more loving and affectionate. She saw that he wanted to make love, so after a quick nightcap they'd gone upstairs. But before he'd half undressed he sat down in the bedside armchair, looking ill. A queer pain in the chest, he said.

I thought he'd eaten too much; and smoked salmon never agreed with him. But soon I saw it was more than that. I helped undress him and put him to bed. In the morning he went into hospital, but didn't come out alive. Before he died he whispered to me, 'I love you Matilda... We do love each other, don't we?' And I said how could he ever doubt it and called him dearest. He said, 'Whatever happens, no regrets eh?' And I said no regrets, Henry, none at all, because that's what he wanted to hear. He told me how I'd given him a new lease of life, taught him what it was all about, that he'd been an old stick-in-the-mud before we met, and so on...

She went out again to the porch, and looked down on the passing crowds, thinning now as evening set in and the

151

pubs opened and people looked for eating places. A large motor cruiser, the *Lodenek Queen*, revved up her engines for the last trip of the day, out to the islands at the mouth of the estuary where, it was claimed, puffins could be seen.

So now here I am in my lonely shell, a hermit crab in a home not my own, left to me in trust for the family afterwards... divorced from the world about me... Look at 'em all down there, milling around and gazing vacantly... you'd think they'd never seen a seagull or a fishing boat in their lives.

No regrets? Oh yes, Henry, I've plenty of regrets, my dear. It wasn't your fault nor mine, but more and more I regret I ever came to Lodenek or to this house of yours. Often I wish we'd never met. My life was devoted to your family, then to you; it was never my own. When I came here this little town couldn't give me the intellectual scope, the mental companionship I craved for... though I did try hard in those years following your death.

She smiled, a trifle satirically, recalling her past efforts to integrate with the townspeople. As if she had been some alien of a different colour or religion. She'd taken part in local dramatics, playing Joanna in *Dear Brutus* (that eerie, strange play from the author of Peter Pan), and even produced *Blithe Spirit* for the Cornubia Players. She'd served on the Urban District Council for six years: a revelation, but soon a very boring one: drains and public seats and refuse collections – exhilarating entertainment! And she ran her own poetry group on Tuesdays, at which the members all recited their own verses to each other until it was evident that none of them had any real talent. Then there had been the Record Circle, at which, in each others' homes (those of them who had decent record playing machines) she had listened to booming Brahms and drifting Delius and lavish, luscious Rachmaninov. There was also the Lodenek Choral Society under the baton of the Squire, dreamy Mr Devereaux who actually composed music, weird modern twelve-note stuff that none of them could make any sense of... But at least with the Choral he stuck to traditional and tuneful songs. One of Matilda's favourites had been Linden Lea:

152

Other folk make money faster
In the air of dark-roomed towns:
I don't dread a peevish master,
Though no man may heed my frowns...

She hummed it, then sang it loudly in a slightly off-key
voice (which had once been a good one); and people below
smiled and one or two clapped her.

For I be free to go abroad,
Or take again my homeward road
To where for me the apple tree
Do lean down low in Linden Lea.

Had a record of that, with Peter Pears singing it; but
clumsy Mary Tregenza who cleaned for me broke it. Got rid
of her, haven't had a daily help since. Daresay I'm slovenly
now, can't be bothered to clean or put things away. It's true
what they say, after a few years the dust doesn't get any
worse. For so long I used to work hard every day, sweeping
and polishing the house – but what's the point, for one
person and no visitors? When I think... what's happened to
me? Matilda, what the devil's come over you these last
twenty years? Washed up here like a piece of debris, a bit of
wreckwood, a spar of flotsam on the beach...

She hadn't, however, been sorry for herself, not until
recently, anyway. Taking what part she could in the life of
Lodenek had given her the illusion that she was wanted,
even needed, by various people around her, and that helped
fill the gap left by Henry and the children. Gradually,
though, she had realised that she was always apart, an
interloper, someone who in the eyes of the local inhabitants
would always be regarded as a newcomer, a 'foreigner.'
They suffered her presence, even voted for her when she
stood for the Council, but there was no warmth or real
contact.

Cornish people said to be hospitable. Well, yes; but then I
rejected anything savouring of pity. I suppose they regarded
me as the grand lady of Priory House, so I got no invitations
into their homes. Perhaps I should have invited them here.
They only call on me when they're collecting for something.

153

People never speak when I go out shopping. Bank clerks, shop assistants, afraid to enquire how I am. Suppose I look strange to them... Ought to brush and comb my hair more, perhaps even put on a bit of make-up. Mend my stockings.

She regarded the long tear down the thigh and across the knee of one of her old grey lisle stockings, one of six pairs she had bought goodness knows how long ago – back in the fifties, probably. You couldn't get lisle now, and she detested nylon.

Why should I care, though? Why should I consider any of 'em? What do they care about me? I did once have Alwyn and Alicia Reece, from the Music Circle, and we played records, but I could see they suffered, listening to my scratchy old stuff. Him with his L.P.'s and stereo equipment. Prissy little accountant. Alicia equally diminutive and smart, like a cut-glass figurine. Always thought them an ideal couple, until he went off what that big bosomy creature, what was her name, Marcia – yes, Marcia Porterhouse, who ran the fashion shop two doors along the quayside here. Scandal, terrific sensation; the old Methodist town not used to such goings-on then...

She stared as the *Pride of Cornwall,* another gleaming white motor cruiser, returned to vomit its bellyful of gawping holidaymakers onto the quayside steps below Priory House. Apart from the small local fishing fleet and a dredger sucking up limesand to sell to farmers, there was little commercial activity in Lodenek port these days.

Back then, in the late fifties and early sixties, still some cargo boats called. Coal and timber and cement. Used to discharge in the Railway Dock, or along the north jetty when the big red brick warehouse was there: delightful continental Dutch sort of design. They tore that down to build holiday flats. Got an old photo somewhere of the cellars under this house when they were used for baking: communal cloam ovens, big round clay things; they lit fires inside, then raked out the red hot ashes and put in pasties and cakes and bread – and roast joints when they could afford such things, which wasn't often. Eighteen-nineties or before. Wives and girl servants tripping across the quayside in long white aprons carrying straw bags – frails they called 'em. Herrings ten a penny then; old Tom Curgenven told me you could smell 'em frying all over the town. That upper storey of the Shipwright's pub, now a classy sea food restaurant, used to be old Clemen's sail loft before the first war. Coal and timber store underneath it when we first came here. Good honest smelly work port then. That was a grain warehouse across the harbour, Martyn and Henwood, where schooners and brigantines used to berth, bringing in the corn from Canada; bagged and unloaded on the quayside, hoisted up to the top floors by pulley. Now it's an hotel, rather upmarket: crab sandwiches, scampi, lasagne, chicken and French fries. Just look at it all now, round the quayside and up the main street: tourists, trippers, dog mess, fish-and-chips, ice-cream, fudge, tropical seashells, knick-knacks and fol-de-rols, obscene T-shirts printed while you wait... What next, I ask myself, what can they do next to this lovely old port?

As she stood there a young woman came up the steps, and with a slightly hesitant smile, said 'Good afternoon, Mrs Marshall.' She carried a pink wallet file stuffed with papers, and had a quietly purposeful air about her. The sort of young married person one might find running a business or behind a bank counter: efficient, pleasant, attractive. She spoke with an educated local accent. Matilda, astounded that anyone should actually accost her, stood there dumbfounded and simply stared at her.

'May I have a word with you? It's quite urgent.' As Matilda still did not react the woman came up to the balcony porch and took from her folder a sheet of paper half-covered with signatures. 'I'm sorry to disturb you, Mrs Marshall, but this is something that surely must concern you. It's a petition we're asking everyone to sign, in protest against the Amusement Arcade the people at the café next door want to establish. Here, right next to Priory House.'

Matilda frowned and held her in her steel-grey, searching stare. 'Amusement Arcade? What's that?'

'Well,' said the young woman, explaining as if to a child, 'they'll have various electronic machines you put money in to gamble with, or to play new games they've invented. It's bound to attract a lot of youngsters here, and we think it would be detrimental to the atmosphere of the whole quayside. What's more, it would be morally bad for the town.'

Matilda gave out a curious mirthless noise, something between a laugh and a snort. 'They've practically ruined Lodenek already, if you ask me, young lady. And if it means getting rid of the fish-and-chips from next door, I'm not sure that I should personally be too upset about it.'

'But surely you wouldn't want young punks with pink hair and half-shaved heads coming in on motorbikes, right outside your door, would you?'

'Might be a change from seeing overweight women and men's hairy bellies parading outside.'

'Of course, it wouldn't be just in summer, you know. It would go on through the winter too. We feel also, the Committee...' She paused, realising that in her eagerness to recruit a new ally she'd forgotten to introduce herself. 'I should explain that I'm Joan Hicks, the secretary of the Committee we've set up to oppose this proposal... We feel that if we're to beat it on planning grounds, the fact that it's next to the oldest house in Lodenek must be our main argument. And if you could personally make an objection in writing on those grounds, our cause would be very much strengthened.'

Matilda turned to look down at the quayside. A young boy carrying a blaring transistor passed obliviously among the ice-cream lickers and chip-eaters. 'I shall have to think about this. Don't want to, of course. Don't want to concern myself with any of your modern nonsense out there.'

'Perhaps,' said Joan Hicks, carefully, 'I can come back tomorrow. Would you mind if I brought our Chairman, Mr Sleeman? He's a Councillor and a Harbour Commissioner. We're hoping to raise money to pay a barrister to represent our case at the Inquiry, in October.'

'I... don't know.' Matilda was genuinely bewildered. 'I'm not good at meeting people any more. Not used to talk, arguing, discussing, not now.'

Once, yes, she would have welcomed the opportunity for political action. Politics with a small p. But now, when her privacy was threatened, it was something that frightened her. A deep terror of other people and of their world impinging upon her haven, the interior emigration she had made, rose up in her.

The young woman was visibly touched. 'We really don't want to impose on you, Mrs Marshall. But you see, we do feel this is so important... and if it happens I'm sure you'll be the first to suffer from it. You probably don't realise the full consequences. As to your objection, we could draft it out for you to sign, if you wish...'

Matilda felt unable to argue any further. She simply had to be rid of this busybody, soft-spoken and sympathetic though she might be. 'Oh very well. I just don't want to be bothered by all this. I suppose I ought to sign. But you can't turn the clock back, you know!' She finished on a sharp schoolmistressly note, the wild stare returning to her eyes.

'We can at least try to stop things getting worse,' Joan said gently. 'You'll sign the petition, then?' She held out the form, affixed to a board, and handed Matilda a pen.

'Where?'

'Just here, under the last name.'

'Very well.' Matilda scrawled her name.

'And the address... no, I can put that in. Thank you, Mrs Marshall. Now – shall I come again with Mr Sleeman?'

'No,' said Matilda. 'No. You can write out the letter for me to read. Perhaps I'll sign it. Perhaps not.' Where was all this leading? What was she letting herself in for? Something Henry had said about reading the small print, on insurance policies and other documents, came back to her.

'Will there be... any small print on it?'

'Oh no. It will be very clear, I promise you. We shall explain everything. I assure you this is in all our interests.' Joan Hicks hesitated before adding, 'Is there... anything I can do for you?'

'Do?' echoed Matilda. A black wrath sprang up in her. 'Do for me? What should there be?'

'I don't know. If I can help in any way...'

'Nobody,' declared Matilda with a grand hauteur, 'does anything for me. I don't need help, young lady, thank you. Now will you go? I must rest after all this...'

'Thank you. I'll get the letter written.' Joan departed after a final glance at Matilda, who stood there now rigid, her eyes closed and fists clenched.

It was too much. The first real contact with anyone in the town for years, and look what it threatened to bring: the entire disruption of her life, her beloved retreat, the devoted solitude which, she now realised, had eaten into her like a spiritual cancer and was now so much a part of her that, if uprooted, it would kill her. She shambled back inside, nausea and dizziness assailing her, and collapsed into the old sagging leather armchair with a broken arm: the result of George fighting in it with Clarissa one day so long ago.

Oh my God. What else, what can there be next? Henry, Henry, what have you consigned me to? I think I'll end it all. Somehow I must... end it...

For the first time in her life suicide now seemed possible, even attractive. Why go on in face of such threats? It wasn't enough to cut yourself off from modern idiocies, to distance yourself and observe them passing by: sooner or later they would turn on you, pursue you into the inner sanctum of your life and thoughts. No escape. She couldn't sell the house and move to some quiet district, even if she could bring herself to do it, the place being entailed for the children after her. She had nowhere else to go.

I could walk out onto the cliffs, throw myself into Tregudda Gorge. One night, perhaps. Nobody would see. I can't stand this. Who is there to turn to? Consult the family solicitor, I suppose; yes, Passmore... but he's in London. A local firm? They'd laugh at me behind their hands and take my money with a straight face. Little enough to spare for litigation, anyway. This Sleeman. He's the port pilot, I think. Perhaps I should talk to him. A Lodenek man, after all. Our interests should coincide, as she said.

She now considered Joan Hicks, and began to feel ashamed of the way she had spoken to her.

158

Nice young woman, why was I so short with her? So rude? Matilda, you were downright *rude*. Deserve to have your face slapped. She took it so well, too. They all humour me, of course... I know what they say in Newquay on the coach tours. Take a trip to Lodenek and see (among other things) the mad woman. I wonder am I really mad after all. No, no, surely only superficially, by their standards. But now... this thing... it really could drive one over the edge. Into the abyss of insanity and despair. O Henry, Henry, what can I do, where can I go? Write to Edward? No, he wouldn't want to be bothered. But surely it's in all their interests too, the house will pass to them...

As she lay there in the chair, staring vacantly up at the cracked and veined ceiling, she became aware that the record was still on the turntable, though the clockwork had run down. The heavy head holding the wooden needle still rested on it.

Must take it off. Won't do the needle any good.

She got up clumsily; as she stood her left leg gave way and she pitched forward on to the floor. A dull pain throbbed in her thigh and spread up her left side to her armpit. She gasped, and drew in harsh throaty breaths. Nausea came in waves and almost choked her.

Aaaaaagh! What have I done? My leg gave way. Can't move... I'm ill... Can't... get up...

A numbness now began to invade her left leg and hip. She was aware of a wetness down her right thigh and leg.

I've peed myself. Whatever is it? A stroke? I've wet the carpet. O dear God... I may not actually believe in you, just an expression... but this is too much. No, dammit, they will not get the better of me. Matilda will... rise again, fight for her rights. As she did... at Girton, fifty years ago...

Struggling to turn herself around, she saw within reach a cushion which had fallen off the armchair, and managed to grab it with her right hand (the left was now beginning to become numb) and place it under her head.

There. Ah. Better now. Very well, just lie here for a while. More or less comfortable. Must consider... what to do...

Gradually she calmed, her breathing becoming easier. In

her abrasive, droning voice she began to whisper hoarsely now, resuming the perpetual monologue going on in her head as she saw through the window the signs of declining day.

Moon rising. White peerless goddess, here she comes. Floating up above the harbour... Evening wanes. Duck egg sky, purple trailers... Quiet outside now. Most of them eating in cafés or pubs. Would that arcade do so much harm? The sheer bother to me of opposing it, rather than the difference it might make... May not be much longer now for me. Hospital, nursing home. O moon, Diana, chaste huntress of the sky, what's to become of me?

Suddenly she shivered, a long racking shudder which, however, quickly ceased, to be succeeded by a cold clammy feeling stealing all over her.

Ought to have had the telephone put in, but seemed so little use for it... Hang a notice from the window, 'HELP'? Pens in bureau, can't drag myself into next room and back... impossible... Matilda, you're caught. Like a lobster in a pot. If she'd only come back with Councillor Sleeman... tomorrow, perhaps, but can I wait that long? I think, I do really think, my time has come. Well, if it must be, it must be. Who's that? Something... someone...

A faint soundless movement in the gathering dusk had made itself known to her, subtly and almost surreptitiously: over in the corner by the window an indistinct shape seemed to appear. One of the presences, the shades with which she had become, in a sense, familiar. She spoke sharply to it.

'Who's there? I can see you... Who are you?'

The shape wavered, gained definition, took the wraithlike form of a young girl or woman in a long dress and apron and a tight bodice. It approached Matilda timidly, as if seeking something of her, as though perhaps it wanted in desperation to appeal to her. Then the whispering voice spoke.

''Tis only me, madam. You've seen me before. I live in the room above yours. I've been here since... O so long ago... Time means nothing to me, existing in everlasting loneliness... I was a servant here to Mr Rouncevall, may he be

160

cursed for my troubles...'

'Aha,' said Matilda with satisfaction. 'Got you in the family way, did he. I knew it.' Her voice softened a little now. 'What's your name, child?'

'Cheston. Cheston Courtnay.' The vision strengthened, acquired more definition with growing confidence, as if reassured that Matilda would be sympathetic. The bodice, Matilda now saw, was old and torn, the skirts unkempt and ragged. The great dark eyes were wells of beseeching in the ghostly face. 'We were of good family once, but fallen from our true estate. My grandfather it was, in the time of Queen Elizabeth, who drank and gambled the property away.' A long echoing sigh followed that statement.

'Well, then, Cheston,' said Matilda, quite kindly. 'What's to be done?'

'I took my own life, madam, they buried me outside the churchyard in unconsecrated ground. So I cannot rest. If someone could get a priest here to bless me, I am sure I should find repose at last.'

'As to that,' Matilda said, thinking of the other apparition she had got used to seeing, 'what about the Reeve, or whoever he is? Can't he bless you?'

A hollow, slightly booming voice spoke from behind her. 'That, madam, I cannot do.' The Reeve himself now appeared, bowing slightly, his portly form in a grey habit already much more definite and solid than Cheston's. 'I should be blaspheming to presume to do such a thing, although I was indeed in Holy Orders.'

'Ah,' Matilda greeted him as an old friend and sparring partner. 'I wondered if you'd appear. Your dog as well, I see.' Behind the Reeve she saw the black and white spaniel, its eyes staring at her, pearly white in the gloom now pervading the room. 'Well, if I'm to go now, it'll make a cosy end for me. Nice little family circle, eh? You're my only family, you know. I've always wanted to talk to you both.' Then, demandingly, 'Why can't you bless her, though?'

'Because,' the deep sepulchral voice resonated, 'I too am damned, as you would say... Sentenced to this limbo for sins much worse than hers. Poor Cheston, I meet her drifting like

161

a skein of sea mist through the house; do you think I would not help her if I could? No, I too am in sore need of blessing.'

'What the devil,' inquired Matilda, 'did you do that was so terrible?'

A strange rusty creaking sound came from the Reeve. She realised he was sighing. 'Too many things, God help me. I was in a position of great trust, here in this house... The office of Portreeve was responsible only to the Prior at St Petroc's in Bodmin. As you surmised, my duties were to collect the money coming into this port. There was the temptation to line my own pockets and, worse, to descend into drunkenness and gluttony... And then at my command certain servants, who knew more than I wanted them to, were quietly disposed of, as you might say. O if ever a man was sinful and dissolute it was me... But I have had so much time to regret and repent my doings. I am the least fitted to bless anyone.'

Matilda saw it all. Here were two lost souls locked in a limbo, neither hell nor heaven, yet hell enough here in the desolation of Priory House, unable even to gain absolution because they had no one to confess to. Why had they not spoken to her before? She wondered whether this was merely a dream, or whether perhaps she too was already dead and condemned to join them here forever.

'I see. I wish I could help you. If I were only able to call a priest and lay you both to rest. But you see, I'm as helpless as you are, lying here waiting for death to take me... I wonder if I also shall be relegated to this limbo, another revenant drifting through this house of too many memories...'

But she received an electrifying jolt when yet another voice spoke, and the form of Henry, her husband, began to materialise near the door. 'No, Matilda, not you,' the soft slightly too-precise voice – yes, indubitably Henry's – was saying. 'Not you. You shall join me in another life. I promise you that, my only true love. On the other side I've been waiting for you. It won't be long now, my dearest.'

'Oh Henry, Henry,' Matilda moaned, her voice choking with love and longing. Until now the possibility of being reunited with him had never been contemplated by her sceptical over-educated mind. 'It is you, isn't it? Yes, I can see it's you.' No doubt about his familiar serious face, only a trifle paler than in life, his solemn trusting eyes. 'Oh my dear, shall we truly be together again? Dare I hope for such a thing after all my cynicism and faithlessness? Don't I too deserve damnation as an agnostic, a heretic?'

The form came a little nearer, bending down towards her. 'We see things very differently from this side. We come and visit you so often. You don't realise we're all about you, especially when you sleep. Even the Reeve and poor Cheston can be freed if they wish. The means are to hand.'

'Oh yes,' the eager, desperate voice of the girl came, rising now above a whisper to an imploring gasp, 'free me, free me! Haven't I paid for my sins over and over?'

Henry turned to her, a magistrate delivering judgement. 'If you choose to regard them as sins they will indeed hang about you for all eternity. Matilda herself can set you free.'

'How is this?' demanded the Reeve. 'Can you really help, madam?' His voice was wistful and longing. 'I should be so eternally grateful to rest after these centuries of desolation.'

Matilda's mind struggled with the prospect of helping them. A deadening weariness, combined with the inexorable cold now creeping over her, held her thoughts back. The chill clammy sleep of death... was it upon her at last? she thought, it's upon me at last. 'I don't know... I'm so tired, and so cold... How shall I do it, Henry?'

'One final effort, my love.' Henry's voice was strong, resolute. 'Bless them both. Give your love and absolution to them. We must all forgive each other, or conscience will hound us for the rest of time.'

Matilda thought, it's as I believed all along. God is imminent and immanent in each one of us. We're all priests, if only we believe in ourselves. 'Very well,' she said, 'Cheston, draw near.'

The girl moved towards her and knelt down. In her dreamlike state Matilda made the sign of the cross over the pallid forehead. 'In the name of Love, the ultimate holiness, I forgive you. Rest now from all your troubles. *In nomine Jesu*

163

Christum Dominum Nostrum.' The Latin came easily, surprising her. Where had she learned that? From some medieval mystery play, probably, which she had studied at Cambridge.

Cheston stood up and wavered into the background.

'Now you, Master Reeve, and your faithful dog.' The Reeve drew near and, as Cheston had, knelt before her with bowed head. Matilda signed the cross over him. 'I absolve you in the name of the human race, for no sin is ultimately unforgivable. You also I love, and invoke the love of your Redeemer to pardon you. *In nomine Jesu Christum Dominum Nostrum, requiescat in pacem.'*

The Reeve stood up, his face transfigured.

'Thank you, madam... I feel such peace now,' Cheston's voice came from beyond him, as her form lost definition and became blurred. 'Peace to you also...'

'I feel so much lighter... insubstantial...' The Reeve's voice was higher, less resonant now. 'May you also rest in peace...' His form began to disperse. 'Eternal thanks to you, dear lady...' His voice was a mere whisper as he melted slowly into the surroundings and finally vanished.

'They're gone. Where have they gone, Henry?' Matilda fixed her eyes on the form of her husband who, at least, still stood by, regarding her with his solemn intent gaze.

'To join us on the Other Side, where perpetual sunshine and summer reign, if we desire them. They will now begin their purification and progress towards a true spiritual life. You have much to learn, my love. I am ready to introduce you to a world you never suspected.'

'Ah,' breathed Matilda, accepting this new conception as Gospel truth, 'take me... take me with you now!'

'That journey we must all undertake alone. But I shall be waiting for you, my dearest.' His voice too was now fading, and his aspect wavering. 'I shall... be waiting...'

'Henry... don't leave me!'

But he too was gone. In the darkening evening the room assumed an exhausted, desolate air. It had become an empty vault. Matilda's mind became a confused swirling of

164

feelings at several removes – grief, anxiety, perplexity. Had those apparitions simply been a dream? Was she wandering in her wits, or had they been true presences she had seen and talked to? Much of it made sense, however: surely everyone needs forgiveness. Forgiveness, she saw, was the only way to peace of mind and spirit.

She had need of it herself. She forgave Sophie, Edward, Clarissa and George for their neglect of her. She forgave the people of Lodenek for ignoring her, even the tourists for laughing at her. And in a last surge of far-off emotion she asked Someone, Something, to forgive her for her harsh thoughts to the world about her.

Then a great black wave of weariness now seemed to bear her down; she could feel nothing of her body, neither arms nor legs. She contemplated what she could still see of the outside world through the window. The moon had risen too high now to be seen. Her thoughts rambled on in poetic disorder.

Only the white sheen of roofs now opposite across the harbour. Green glow for starboard, red for port; lights out on the piers. My ship coming home to anchor. All at peace, nothing to shatter the calm. Lodenek becomes itself again. As it was and as it shall be... Evermore? Nevermore? All silly amusements shall whirl away like postcards in the wind, insubstantial fripperies passing in a twinkle of God's eye. Where are those eternal truths I once sought? All that reading, studying, thinking, where has it got me in the end? Here, dying on the floor with nobody to care.

But Henry was waiting for her. He would receive her in a new world and conduct her into its mysteries. She was convinced, with a radiant certainty now, that this was not the end. She looked at the things she had loved and collected, and said a soft farewell to her books and records, her little pictures and newspaper cuttings, her china dogs and vases, her collections of stones and shells. Red for port, green for starboard; she was coming home to port at last.

I'm coming, Henry... coming, my dearest... coming...

Outside the moon mounted higher and curlews began to call across the sand bars of the estuary.

GLOSSARY OF NON-ENGLISH PHRASES

Page

12   *In Nomine Patris et Filius et Spiritus Sancti*: In the name of the Father and the Son and the Holy Spirit.
Miserere, yn yffarn, etc.: Have mercy, in hell I am. André Robert is my name. Help me, do help me, I pray   you... pray you...

16   *Aidez-moi. Gwer dhym*, etc: Help me. Help me. Help, please. I cannot die. I want to die. I'm guilty. Help me, I pray you.

17   *Mort, vous êtes vraiment*, etc.: Dead, you are truly dead. Do you understand?
Si je suis mort... etc.: If I am dead, why have I no rest? I am in Hell. In Hell, but it is cold, it is not hot here.
Faîtes-vous confession etc.: Make your confession. Pray for absolution.
Je ferai confession pour mes péchés: I will make confession for my sins.
Méchant nous somes tous... etc.: We are all wicked. We are all sinners... damned, damned!

Douze. Deudhek, etc.: Twelve. Twelve... My woman. The old woman also. Sinners all, all. We have killed. We have killed.

22   *J'ai tué. Yn wyr*: I have killed. In truth.
Mais oui: But yes.
Hep dowt: Without doubt.
Pardonnez-moi, A Dhew etc.: Pardon me, O God in the highest. Let me rest!

22/23 *In nomine*, etc.: see above. *Ego te absolvat*: I absolve you.

134 *Dysqua dhyn-ny dha nerth, Dewes Vur*: Show us your power, great Goddess.
Canen gans oll agan gallos: Let us sing with all our might.

135 *Deugh, deugh*, etc.: Come, come...
Deugh dhyn-ny, etc.; Come to us, come the Matres, Great Lugh and the Dagda also, all come to us.

136 *Gans tan*, etc.: With fire make ready sacrifice; To our gods we give it.

GLOSSARY OF NON ENGLISH PHRASES (Contd.)

Page

136 *Deugh dh'agas tuatha,* etc.: Come to your people, gods great and Celtic. Take our sacrifice, we pray you.
Epona, Epona ro, etc.: Epona, give us blessing, and blessing to our dead ancestors.

137 *Epona, Epona gwyth,* etc.: Epona, Epona, keep from us all evil.
Nemetona, etc.: Nemetona, Nemetona, great goddess of our battles, keep from us the devil, and do harm to our enemies.

138 *Gwra kerensa,* etc.: Create love, create prosperity, Cernunnos our God –

163/4 *In Nomine...* etc.: In the Name of Jesus Christ our Lord.

164 *In Nomine,* etc.: see above. *Requiescat in pacem*: Rest in peace.